A FRIEND in the DARK

A FRIEND in the DARK

PASCAL RUTER

Translated by Emma Mandley

WALKER
BOOKS

First published in Great Britain 2017 by Walker Books Ltd
87 Vauxhall Walk, London SE11 5HJ

2 4 6 8 10 9 7 5 3 1

Text © Didier Jeunesse, Paris, 2012
English translation © 2017 Emma Mandley
Cover design © 2017 Walker Books Ltd

The translator would like to thank The Panhard et Levassor Club GB
and The English Chess Federation for their invaluable help.

The right of Pascal Ruter and Emma Mandley to be identified as author
and translator respectively of this work has been asserted by them in
accordance with the Copyright, Designs and Patents Act 1988

This book has been typeset in Joanna

Printed and bound in Great Britain by Clays Ltd

British Library Cataloguing in Publication Data:
a catalogue record for this book is available from the British Library

ISBN 978-1-4063-7260-1

www.walker.co.uk

"I would rather walk with a friend in the dark
than alone in the light."

Helen Keller

This story takes place in a village in France, a few miles south of Paris...

1

The alarm clock rang. One second later I heard Dad come up the stairs and fling open my bedroom door.

"Come on, get up, today's the big day!"

He gave me a shake.

"Get a move on, you're going to be late!"

He bounded back downstairs. During the holidays, I'd completely forgotten about the morning rush to get ready — and today, the first day of a new school year, my brain felt full of fog. I could hear Dad bustling about downstairs, getting breakfast ready. The familiar sounds were just rocking me gently back into a deep sleep when he yelled, "Are you going to get up or do I need to get a crane to lift you out?"

I jumped and sat up in bed, tentatively stretching one foot out, as if I was dipping it into cold water.

Then I randomly grabbed some trousers and a T-shirt. Oh well, so much for looking stylish. My feet felt like lead as I went downstairs.

In the kitchen, Dad had made me a hot chocolate. The warm, comforting smell helped lift the fog in my head a little.

"Have you got all your stuff together?" he asked, raising his eyebrows as high as they would go and waggling his right hand as if he was massaging my head from the other side of the room. I tried to look as if I had everything under control.

"Yes, I think so, but ... you can't always be sure ... can you?"

He washed up a couple of cups and, before going back to bed, he said, "Don't forget to shave off your chocolate moustache. It's important to look your best!"

I ambled into the living room. The sun was just coming up and it shone into the little yard. A few fallen leaves were lying on the ground like dried butterflies. It was getting late, so I went to find my rucksack. It looked very small and battered. This year I wasn't going to let myself be intimidated by the problems that lurked inside it. I rummaged around and found the list of school equipment I was supposed to have bought. I'd forgotten to give it to Dad. Too late now. Still, he might have thought of it himself: isn't that how it's supposed to work, when you're part of a team?

I nearly charged into his room to tell him, but in the end I didn't bother... I began to empty my rucksack to assess the situation. I unearthed some pencil ends and a picture of an apple tree with big red apples lying all around its trunk: one of my friend Haisam the Honourable's bizarre drawings. I hesitated, but then I stuck it to the wall. What had he been trying to tell me? As a general rule, I don't understand either his drawings or anything he says, and if I ask him to explain it's even worse. I also found my last paper for Year Eight – with a mark of 2 out of 10 and the comment "Some progress" – as well as a photo of a woman in a swimsuit, torn out of a magazine. The swimsuit was quite revealing, though there wasn't all that much to reveal. I shook the rucksack to make sure it was completely empty: there's something hopeful about making a fresh start.

Now it felt oddly light. Obviously, a rucksack with nothing in it seems a bit pointless, but I managed to make it heavier with a couple of blank exercise books that had been languishing at the bottom of a drawer since last year. So far, my school prospects weren't looking all that much better, despite the resolutions I'd made about getting my things more organized.

I had to adjust the rucksack's straps and let them out a bit, because they were cutting into my shoulders. It felt like I'd grown, so I went to check in the long mirror. It was true, I'd filled out quite a lot. I was pleased, because among other things, it's important in life to have a good physique.

Before leaving, I called out a half hearted "Bye!". As I'd expected, there was no answer from Dad. It wasn't his fault. He must have got back from Paris very late. As usual, he'd been really careful not to wake me, and now he needed to catch up on his sleep.

It wasn't too cold, just a bit grey. Dad's old car, a 1960s Panhard, was parked in the paved yard. Dad was obsessed with that car. He'd spent the whole of the previous day adjusting the rocker arms and he'd had terrible problems with the oil feed. I'd suggested refitting the oil feed pipe last, and it had done the trick. After I'd gone to bed, Dad had set off on his deliveries – the M10S engine thrumming beautifully as the car started. It was the perfect lullaby.

* * *

When I got to school there were people everywhere. I walked past the caretaker's lodge but Haisam wasn't there and nor was his father, the caretaker. So I went to join the other kids in the playground, where we were supposed to assemble while we waited for the head teacher.

The playground was crowded and some of the parents, who were behind the railings, stuck their heads through the bars, trying to catch a glimpse of what was happening. They were holding on to them with both hands, like prisoners desperate for a sniff of freedom. It was a strange view of the world. The head teacher arrived and began to call out our names. One by one we got into line in front of our form teachers. And when everyone in a class had been called, the form teacher led them inside. Whole processions of children disappeared in this way, and little by little the playground emptied. I was wondering where on earth Haisam the Honourable could have got to, when I felt a hand on my shoulder. I didn't need to turn around to know it was him.

"Honourable Egyptian," I murmured, "I hope we're going to be in the same class."

"It's sorted."

So then I turned round, because I was eager to

see his face again. He seemed to have got even fatter over the holidays. His great stomach was stuffed into a massively uncool, thick checked shirt and he was wearing corduroy trousers that were much too short, revealing different coloured socks. His small eyes were smiling behind his ever-present horn-rimmed specs. He had the calm, unruffled look of someone who's seen it all before. I've never understood how Haisam could be so impervious to the world of fashion, but hey, that's his business. I was nudged in the ribs by a sharp Egyptian elbow.

"Victor! Absent? Absent already?" The head teacher was yelling through her megaphone.

This really wasn't the moment to make her think I'd bunked off: I didn't want to draw attention to myself right at the beginning of the year. Better to wait a little.

"No! No! I'm here," I shouted, waving my arms wildly. "I'm coming, look, I'm getting in line!"

A little later Haisam came to join me in the queue. He'd said, "It's sorted," and it was. We trudged through the corridors behind our form teacher. I didn't know anyone else in the class but maybe that was a good thing, if I wanted to keep a low profile.

We sat down at our desks and the teacher asked

14

us to fill in a form with our personal details, because at the beginning of the year "they" wanted to know something about us. I've never understood quite why, but anyway... Actually I would have liked to know more about the teachers, but I'd never raised it, because coming from me it would probably have looked suspicious. But still, it would have been interesting to know where they lived, what their families were like and so on. More interesting than quite a lot of other things.

Haisam, as usual, had sat down in the back row. I'd hoped that he might have had a change of heart, but apparently not; he still wanted to be on his own at the back of the class. He explained that this was because during lessons he entered into a state of deep concentration that could easily be mistaken for sleep. Of course, I knew that it was a sort of essence of concentration – like strong Turkish coffee – but at the beginning of the year the teachers were always fooled by it and thought he was having a snooze. His eyes would be half-closed, his arms crossed over his stomach and sometimes his chin rested on his chest. Haisam said that at times like this he was being a Nile crocodile: he appeared to be asleep but in fact he was soaking up the whole lesson like a sponge. He could react to the teacher's slightest word or tone of voice, just like a croc who seems to be sleeping but can grab anything passing with one snap of its jaws.

Last year the maths teacher was demonstrating the solution to a totally baffling problem on the board, with root thingummies everywhere and formulas that looked like something out of science fiction. While the teacher was scurrying backwards and forwards from one end of the board to the other, my friend the Honourable Egyptian was his usual serene self, peacefully dozing with his chin on his chest, writing nothing down. Then he lifted one eyelid and very politely asked the teacher if he could say something.

"With all due respect, sir, I think there's a simpler way of doing this."

Haisam strolled over to the board and picked up a marker. We all sensed that a miracle might be about to take place. In a little corner of the board he wrote one small, perfect line of figures and symbols. The teacher opened his eyes wide, as though he'd looked through a door and glimpsed infinity.

"You're quite right," he said, in a thin little voice that was both despairing and admiring.

After that he went on sick leave, probably to think a few things over.

On the personal details form, I was wondering what I could put down as "father's profession". I wrote down "buyer", because that's what seemed to fit best. He sold things as well, of course, but I thought that "buyer" sounded more mysterious, and also more distinguished.

Then my mind wandered back to the car. Had Dad remembered to leave 0.15 mm slack on the Panhard's inlet and exhaust valves? If not, the rocker arms were unlikely to last very long. I worried about it for a little while and lost track of what the teacher was saying.

After the last lesson, I met Haisam in the playground. We headed towards the caretaker's lodge, where his father would be waiting for him, sitting at the chessboard, with a pyramid of translucent Turkish delight beside him. It was slow progress, because Haisam never hurried.

I called him Haisam the Honourable because he always introduced himself in the same way, like a recorded message, "I'm Haisam: it's an honourable Egyptian name."

He was a sort of philosopher: once he'd told me that in his opinion the Egyptian pyramids were clear proof that human beings never learn their lesson, and that their natural inclination is to lose heart and get lazier and lazier. I didn't really understand, so that evening I'd asked Dad. At first he'd nearly choked laughing and then he'd advised me to watch out, because Haisam was clearly a pessimist. I'd looked in the dictionary that Dad had given me as an incentive to study and this is what I found:

Pessimism *a tendency to believe that the worst will happen.*

I always liked being the last to leave school – and the last to arrive too for that matter – and Lucky Luke couldn't understand why. (It was Haisam, by the way, who'd pointed out the similarity between the Head of Year and Lucky Luke, the cartoon cowboy.) So that day after school I watched Haisam and his father play chess for a while as the school emptied, lining my stomach with Turkish delight. Haisam moved his pieces very slowly and ceremoniously, like a magician. His father always had a little smile playing on his very thin lips, but the two of them hardly ever spoke to each other during a game. My dear friend took a piece of Turkish delight after each move, chewing slowly while he waited for his father to respond. Before the icing sugar fell on his checked shirt, it floated for a moment above the chessboard. There was something secretive and cosy about the peaceful silence and the little cloud of sugar hiding us from the world. Now and then someone would look into the lodge to ask Haisam's father something, and he would reply with a vague wave of his hand.

There were many mysteries surrounding my friend. How come Haisam was so fat and his father was so thin? And why did he have an Egyptian name when his father was Turkish? And also, above all, why did my noble Egyptian observe the Sabbath, the Jewish day of rest, which didn't seem to be a very Egyptian thing, nor Turkish either for that matter. There were many things about my friend Haisam that I didn't understand. Sometimes I looked in my dictionary, but even then I couldn't always find an answer. So I watched them play chess and stuffed myself with Turkish delight, which is called lokum in Turkish.

Lokum from the Arabic "comfort for the throat". An oriental sweet made from flavoured cubes of jelly dusted with icing sugar.

"So how did it go?" asked my father later, peering out from underneath the bonnet of the Panhard with his face covered in oil. "I hope you kept out of trouble?"

19

I sighed.

"So far…"

He frowned suspiciously. At the end of the previous year he'd promised the school authorities – in particular Lucky Luke – that he'd keep tabs on me. To encourage me, he'd bought me a book called *The Three Musketeers*, by Alexandre Dumas, as well as the dictionary I've already mentioned.

"Did you remember to leave 0.15 mm slack on the Panhard's inlet and exhaust valves?" I asked him. "If not, your rocker arms are done for."

He said nothing and wiped his tools clean.

"Dad…"

"Yes, what?"

"How long do you think it took Alexandre Dumas to write *The Three Musketeers*?"

"I don't know."

"A whole year?"

"Perhaps … but I expect it took him longer."

"Maybe three years? One year for each musketeer?"

"Maybe."

"Another thing, Dad…"

"Yes … hang on, I'm going to sit down, in case you're going to spring something nasty on me."

He plonked himself down on the car's front seat.

"What I'd like to know is... Did you do well at school, in the olden days?"

He looked relieved and smiled, gazing into the distance. He seemed to be searching through his memories. With his right hand he slowly rubbed his chin, as though it was a magic lamp and sparks from the past might shoot out from it.

"Yes, I was completely brilliant!"

"In what subjects?"

"In all of them."

He gave a rather strange smile, proud and a bit sad at the same time. Behind the windscreen his face looked slightly distorted.

I wasn't entirely sure whether to believe him or not, since it's a father's job to set a good example. I went inside. I'd ask Haisam the Honourable about *The Three Musketeers* and Alexandre Dumas. I drank a glass of water before going up to my bedroom in the attic. Then I emptied my rucksack and put the new textbooks away on the shelves that had been specially built for them. I stuck my weekly timetable to the wall, because in Year Eight I'd got the subjects, days and times muddled up and I never had the right books with me. Lastly, I wrote the subject and the name of the teacher on the first page of all my exercise books and covered them with clear plastic. It took quite a long time, but it was good to see them looking so smart and it felt like progress. Progress in my method. And I don't care what anyone says, method is important in life. I went back down to the sitting room and asked Dad if we could cook some Egyptian rice, using the recipe that Haisam had given me.

While we were eating, he asked, "So, young man, are you happy with your teachers this year?"

He sounded so serious that I was alarmed. I could see he was thinking of his promise to Lucky Luke and wanted to check that I was setting off on the right foot from the very start of the year. I nodded firmly to reassure him.

"You see, my boy, it's the beginning of the school year that sets the pace. It's all about how you start. Not too fast, but lively enough. Obviously, you have to watch out you don't get knac— puffed out too quickly."

He put his hand on my shoulder.

"Life, old buddy, is like a cycle race. You have to approach it like the mountain stages of the Tour de France. It's not a time trial. Remember that."

Where on earth did he pick up these sayings? He seemed to be developing as much of an obsession with metaphors as Haisam.

"There are too many hills for me and I keep skidding all over the place. And anyway, Dad, cycling hurts your bum. So no offence, but if you want to encourage me and teach me about life you'll have to come up with a different comparison."

We cleared the table and sat down facing each other in the two deep, shabby armchairs. I began, because I'd lost the previous evening.

"The date of the first Panhard and Levassor three-point engine suspension patent?"

He thought for a few seconds.

"Easy: January the fourteenth 1901. My turn. In what year was the Panhard car first equipped with a radiator?"

I shut my eyes to make it easier to think. First radiator ... first radiator...

"I've got it: 1897. And what's more I can tell you that it was in the Paris–Dieppe motor race."

My father whistled in admiration and got up, because he had work to do.

"I still don't understand how it is that you can learn everything there is to know about the Panhard car by heart, but you can't..."

I could see where this was going, and even if he was right, that didn't make it right.

23

"I get it, Dad. Stop now though, because, well, you know."

"Do you remember when you thought Nelson Mandela was the centre forward for the Auxerre football team?"

"Don't poke fun at me."

We had a good laugh, blowing memories to each other like bubbles.

"You wait," he said, brandishing the Krebs manual, which is a sort of bible covering everything there is to know about the Panhard car. "Tomorrow I'll have a really impossible one for you. You'll never get it."

"I will too. And you won't either."

In my bedroom, I had a quick look at the timetable stuck on the wall and felt a bit depressed. My first lesson the following day was at eight-thirty. I thought again about what my father had said: "It's all about how you start. Not too fast, but lively enough." I saw Alexandre Dumas' book on the bedside table. There was no doubt it was going to take me longer to read than it took him to write. I was at page four. I decided to read the Krebs manual instead, because I really wanted to catch Dad out.

2

$$x - 2(4x + 1) = 4(2 - x) + 2$$

Without a doubt, this was my first problem of the year. Not the only problem, but the first. I tried to remember what we'd learned last year, but frankly nothing came to me. I looked over at Haisam, who'd already put down his fountain pen. I wondered whether for once he didn't know the answer, but it turned out that he'd already finished, thanks to the mysterious turbocharger in his brain. I threw him a despairing look and he just raised his chubby hand a few inches off the desk. That's his way of giving encouragement. What he means is: don't worry, it'll all work out, maybe not so well, but it'll work out. It's true that I was feeling quite anxious, because of my difficulties at school and the gaps in my knowledge.

I stole a glance at the maths teacher, who made a funny sound when she walked because she was lame. In fact sometimes she could only get around with the help of two crutches. They ticked and tocked as though she was using them to measure the passing of time. Haisam, who always knew everything, had told me that she was very unhappy because she'd lost a baby a long time ago. I thought that probably explained why she was now making us do equations. One day I'd asked Haisam if he thought she was still carrying the dead baby in her right leg. He'd given me a funny look, with his mouth wide open, which is always a sign that he's thinking deeply. Then he'd put his hand on my shoulder.

"Maybe there's hope for you still, my friend."

My remark seemed to have made quite an impression on him and from that moment on he took me a bit more seriously. It felt cool to think he saw me as someone to be reckoned with.

I pretended to be writing and tried not to get myself noticed. Luckily, the bell rang.

It was the last lesson and Haisam took his time putting his things away in his locker. I hung around for a bit, but since he didn't show up I went ahead to his father's lodge. That day he was wearing his splendid red fez hat, which made him look like a nobleman from the olden days. I was hypnotized by the little golden tassel that hung from a velvet ribbon, fastened to the top of the fez.

I grabbed the opportunity of my Honourable Egyptian's absence to try and clear up some of the mysteries that were puzzling me.

"Sir," I asked, "could you please explain to me why you chose an Egyptian name for Haisam – well, he wasn't called Haisam until you named him that obviously – when you're Turkish? And also, I'd really like to know why you observe the Sabbath on Friday nights?"

"When do you think we should observe it? On Wednesday mornings? Or on Monday afternoons?"

He smiled and I could see that he was making fun of me.

"What I mean is, the Sabbath isn't really a Turkish sort of thing, nor Egyptian actually…"

He raised his hand in a slightly limp way that reminded me of Haisam.

"Who knows! Who knows…"

Haisam arrived at last. I asked him to explain the maths to me, because well … equations! We settled down at the back of the lodge so as not to be disturbed.

"What is it you want to know?" he asked.

He seemed very calm.

"Well, I want to know what you're supposed to do with this gibberish: $x - 2(4x + 1) = 4(2 - x) + 2$. It's not that I've got anything against maths, but still, really."

"It's not very hard. Start by multiplying it out."

He stuffed an enormous piece of Turkish delight in his mouth and began to chew slowly and deliberately, with a strange gleam in his eyes.

"Multiplying out what?" I asked.

"Well, the brackets of course. What else would you want to multiply out?"

"I don't understand."

"Right. You cross out the brackets and that gives you: $x - 8x - 2 = 8 - 4x + 2$. See?"

"Then what do I do? That's not all, is it?"

"Of course not, you dope. Then you put all the xs on the left and everything else on the right. And don't forget to swap the plus signs to minus when they switch sides."

"OK, so that makes… that makes… $x - 8x + 4x = 8 + 2 + 2$."

"And there you are. So now what do we do?"

"I don't know, maybe we could go and kick a ball around!"

He nearly choked on his Turkish delight. There was icing sugar coming out through his eyes: they looked like two little snowballs.

"No, you birdbrain, you haven't finished it. You've got to find the value of x!"

I felt tears come into my eyes. I thought of Dad, who had given me *The Three Musketeers*, who had done super well at school when he was young, who'd had his ear chewed off by Lucky Luke and who did everything, pretty much, to keep tabs on me ... and here I was, KO'd by the first x of the year.

"Right," Haisam resumed calmly. "You need to simplify. So simplify."

"OK, I'm simplifying, I'm simplifying. I'll simplify until it's simply fizzing. Here we are, I get: $-3x = 12$."

"And now you just need to divide by 3!"

"Obviously... Whew! But it looks a bit weird to me: $x = 12 \div -3...$ I must have slipped up somewhere..."

"No, it's right, it means $x = -4$. Do you get it now?"

"To be honest, I don't really see the point of it, but I get it. Though I don't know if I'll be able to do it again on my own. I can't promise."

"I can't think how you're going to manage an equation with several unknowns," he said, guzzling another piece of Turkish delight.

"Is there such a thing?"

"In maths, everything's possible."

"How come you learnt all this?"

"It's different for me. I can't claim any credit for myself: Egyptians have always been great mathematicians."

"What about Turks who observe the Sabbath?"

"Turks too. Even those who don't observe the Sabbath."

The following week, things got complicated. Things have a natural tendency to get complicated, I find. First of all, the geography teacher got mad at me when he was giving back our work because for the question about the climate in the South of France, I'd answered that "there is snow and sometimes low tide". I understood what I meant, but I was certainly the only one who did. The whole class burst out laughing, especially a group of snotty, stuck-up girls who look like they're reciting a mathematical theorem when they laugh. I bet their farts don't even smell. Even Haisam smiled, but in his case it was just friendly affection.

I'd forgotten to revise the stuff on the climate because of the piston pins. Dad had wanted to replace the old five ring pistons with modern four groove ones, so he'd had to dismantle the whole engine and take out the chrome pins. I'd fetched the Krebs manual from my room and we'd looked it up. We'd realized that we'd need to check the connecting rod and cylinder to avoid the pistons jamming, because you know what that would have led to. Anyway, it was because of all this that I forgot about the climate in the South of France. It's not that I have anything against geography. My Honourable Egyptian's father had shown me where Egypt was on a map, and I'd seen that it was a country with a lot of water everywhere except where there was desert.

"What about Turkey?" I'd asked.

He'd pointed very precisely at a spot on the map that was tacked to the wall. His fingernail, as polished as a pearl, made a little tapping noise.

"There's Turkey. Just there."

"Huh, that's strange, I thought that was India."

During the break, after the geography lesson, I hung around on my own so that I could think about what Dad was going to say and how I could explain my bad mark.

I watched the footballs streaking across the playground and thought to myself that when it came down to it, perhaps I just wasn't cut out for studying. I got the impression that the girls in the class were taking the mick, because they were looking up at the sky and saying loudly, "I wonder when it's going to snow…" And then they snorted with laughter, in a snotty, stuck-up sort of way. Haisam had disappeared and I didn't know where to turn for support. I thought back to my father's test question from last night, "At the time of the 1901 Paris–Berlin motor race, what technical innovations would you have found in the Panhard cars?" I couldn't find the answer even in the Krebs manual.

I felt very downhearted and turned down all invitations to go and play so that I could continue to think things over, which is a very important thing to do in life. I could already picture Dad in the head teacher's office with Lucky Luke tearing a strip off him and that was something I wanted to avoid at all costs, so as not to hurt his fatherly feelings. I also thought again about Alexandre Dumas, who always made a big effort to entertain us and to teach us loads of historic things, even though he never knew us. I promised myself that I would read at least twenty pages of *The Three Musketeers* that evening. Then I dropped it down to fifteen, because it's best to pace yourself so you don't run out of steam.

The bell rang at the end of break and I didn't know if that was a good or a bad thing. Full of misgivings, I got in line to wait for the sports teacher. I thought about Dad and his school record to give myself courage. Sport would get me back on track.

Half an hour later it would be true to say that I was having no more luck with sport than with the climate in the South of France. I'd ended up eyeball to eyeball with Lucky Luke, in his office. He was standing with his legs slightly apart, as if he was squaring up for a duel. He looked as though he was about to pull out a piece of chalk and write "dunce" on my forehead.

"I must say I thought that things had been made absolutely clear and that you'd taken it all on board... Isn't that right? I thought you'd made some resolutions ... that you had good intentions..."

"Yes ... but then again no..."

"What do you mean, yes but then again no?"

"Well, I mean that I did have resolutions, as well as intentions, but words often just slip out on their own..."

"Right, let's recap. The sports teacher gets you all to line up…"

"Yes, and then he goes to fetch the keys to the gym…"

"And everyone's quietly waiting for him in line?"

"Yes, sir, everyone's waiting for him, that's exactly right…"

"And so at that moment you decide to draw attention to yourself. Please could you repeat out loud what you said?"

I scratched my chin. To tell the truth I felt alone in a hostile environment. I asked myself what d'Artagnan in *The Three Musketeers* would have done in this situation.

"You'd like me to repeat…"

"Yes."

"If you're trying to make me feel ashamed, that's not very nice of you."

"Repeat what you said or I'm calling your father!"

He made a big show of grabbing the telephone and looking up the number. I began to panic, because he'd figured out what would get to me.

"So I should repeat it?"

"Yes."

"Well, so there we were waiting in line. Then out

of the blue it started to rain. You know, Monsieur Luc— Monsieur Guénolé, those big drops of summer rain which are like flies banging against dry window panes..."

"Spare me your literary talents."

"All the same, literature is important, isn't it, sir...?"

"I don't give a stuff, I just want you to repeat what you said when you were standing in line."

"Have you read *The Three Musketeers* by Alexandre Dumas, sir?"

"No, I haven't read *The Three Musketeers*... Why? Have you read it?"

"Yes ... well, nearly... Did you know that Alexandre Dumas took three whole years to write that book, one year for each musketeer?"

"No, I didn't know..."

Suddenly, he seemed to pull himself together.

"Right. Come on! I want to know what you said in the line."

"What I said? You really want to know? Well, OK then, when I was in the line I said, 'So what do we do now? Play with ourselves?'"

He said nothing for a few seconds, as though it was taking a while for the words to sink in. I couldn't tell if he was going to smile or burst into tears.

"You disappoint me, young man, you disappoint me. And yet you're not a bad fellow."

"No, sir."

"You could do well…"

"Absolutely, sir. It's mostly a question of method, according to the specialists."

"Do you want to please your father?"

Ouch!

All at once there was a miracle: I remembered the local newspaper that Dad rolled his greasy tools in. A secret weapon. A counter-attack worthy of the musketeer d'Artagnan.

"By the way, sir, I know I'm changing the subject, but congratulations on Sunday's bike race. I really thought the other cyclists would catch you up, but you gave it that one last push…"

Touché. This really was just like *The Three Musketeers*. I'd hit upon the fact that Lucky Luke was also a top-ranking cyclist. All his spare time was spent in the saddle. It was funny to think his bum must always be hurting.

He gave me a strange, slightly suspicious look.

"Were you there?"

"Yes," I said, trying to remember what the

newspaper article had said. "I've never seen a breakaway like that before. Even in the Tour de France. If you want my opinion, you could have been a professional, a real champion."

"Perhaps, but you have to take so much stuff... I never wanted to do that: taking care of one's health is what matters most."

"You were right. Health is important for sure... In my view, the essential thing in a race is not to start too fast, so that you don't run out of steam... It's the same thing with a school year." (I hoped he'd appreciate the comparison.) "Can I go now, because it's getting dark..."

"No more nonsense then, I don't want to hear your name coming up again. No more of that vulgar language. Otherwise I'll have to call your father and he won't be happy."

"You're right about that."

I left his office, but with all that carry-on I'd missed the school bus. From a distance I could see Haisam and his father settling down to a game of chess in the lodge. I felt like going to watch them and stuffing myself with Turkish delight to take my mind off things. There's nothing like chess for that, but I thought I'd better go home, because I'd made enough of a spectacle of myself for one day. The Honourable Egyptian noticed me and raised his big hand in greeting. His horn-rimmed glasses always made him look infinitely serene, like a large placid owl.

I walked home just as the sun was beginning to set behind the trees, along the edge of the little wood that fringed the road. It was there, right in amongst the trees, that our biology teacher kept a little pond where he could observe tadpoles and frogs. Last year, I'd had the bright idea of pouring some washing-up liquid into the water. This killed some of the frogs, which were found floating face-up, and meant the rest failed to develop properly. I swore to Lucky Luke that an amphibian massacre wasn't at all what I'd intended, but he only partly believed me. To make amends and to prove my love of nature, I'd had to look after the pond for half the Christmas holidays. Later in the year, after all that, Monsieur Dubois made us study frogs' reflexes. He dissected one of the creatures and fixed electrodes all over it. So much for the lecture about respect for frogs and love of animals in general, that's all I can say.

I walked on down the hill and passed the big

houses at the entrance to the village. And then just before the church I saw one of the girls in my class. Marie... Marie something, I couldn't remember. I thought about turning back, because to be honest, I'd had enough... But since she was also heading towards the village and I was already late, I just slowed down to avoid catching up with her. In the end it was she who turned round: when she saw me, instead of scuttling off as I'd have expected, she stopped and waved at me. I was trapped.

"Do you think it's going to snow today?" she asked.

"Oh, give it a rest! Don't you ever scr— mess things up?"

She seemed to be thinking, as though weighing up her reply.

"Well, no, actually – I don't."

It didn't look as though being perfect made her particularly happy.

"And anyway it was because of Dad's piston pins, but obviously you wouldn't understand."

"Is that what you think?"

It was going round and round in my head: her name... Marie... Marie... Marie what?

"Definitely, trust me," I replied at last.

I'd put on a serious expression, because at least

39

on the subject of Panhard cars I knew I didn't make mistakes and could even claim to be quite an authority. I was wrong yet again, as it turned out, but that's for later. For a few minutes we couldn't think of anything to say to each other. I was a bit distracted with trying to remember her name... It was on the tip of my tongue, but it kept slipping away. I snatched a glance at her. Her hair was reddish and incredibly curly. It flew around all over the place, hiding half her face. Apart from that, she seemed as neat and tidy as a Japanese doll and I remembered that I hadn't had a shower for three days. I swore I'd have a good scrub that very evening, because self-respect is important. I tried to think of something to say to impress her a bit: the climate issue was bugging me and I have my pride. All at once an idea came to me.

"I've got a question for you... Have you read any books by Alexandre Dumas?"

"The father or the son?"

"What do you mean?"

"Alexandre Dumas the *father*, or Alexandre Dumas the *son*?"

I had no idea what she was talking about: once again things were getting complicated. But I could look into that later. Right now it would be better to change the subject. I tried to think of something that didn't hold too much danger for me. By chance I caught a glimpse of her right hand. She was wearing a big ring, so I thought I'd pay her a compliment.

"That's a superb gallstone you've got on your finger. Is it a real one?"

I couldn't understand why she was looking at me like I was from outer space. She didn't seem to know what to say next, as though we were speaking different languages. So I took the initiative.

"I get the impression you're interested in intellectual things."

She seemed a bit taken aback by this new change of direction and frowned. She must have been wondering if I was trying to catch her out or something.

"Why, aren't you?"

I'd got it at last. Her name was Marie-José.

"Sure," I said with as much conviction as possible, "intellectual things interest me too. Though not all the time."

"For instance, I found the biology lesson on the eye very instructive," she said.

She seemed to be lost in thought. She went on, as though talking to herself. "It's crazy what goes on inside the iris and the cornea…"

"Did you see," I asked, "when he explained how you go blind because of that shi— tricky cornea?"

We were coming up to the baker's and I realized that the sun had disappeared and darkness was beginning to fall gently around us like a veil. She stopped suddenly, turned towards me and said, with a smile in her voice, "When you're blind, you can't see the snow in the South of France or whether the tide's in or out. That would be annoying for you, when you love the area and its climate so much."

She turned her back on me and that was that. I was left feeling utterly humiliated.

Humiliation the action of humiliating or the condition of being humiliated. Impairment to self-esteem. See abasement.

There were at least two words in this definition that I didn't understand. If you have to be a specialist to understand a definition, you might as well give up.

It was still bothering me when I got home, so I asked Dad.

"Dad, seriously, did you know that there were two writers called Alexandre Dumas?"

He was absorbed in the *Journal for Collectors and the Curious*, but he glanced up.

"Yes, father and son."

I sighed deeply and mournfully.

"Why are you sighing like that?"

"Well, it's just that I've realized other people know loads of things that I'm completely in the dark about… On the way back from school I met a girl from my class who already knew that there were two of them. I'll never dare to speak to her again about *The Three Musketeers*: I'm sure she must have read it several times already. And as for Haisam, he must have known about it for years… By the way, why did Alexandre Dumas give his son the same first name as himself?"

"I've no idea. Perhaps he wanted him to write books too and thought the name would bring him luck."

"It's an odd thing to do. The one who wrote *The Three Musketeers*, was that the father or the son?"

"The father."

"I thought so…"

"Thought what?"

"I thought that it seems more like a book written by a father than by a son."

It was getting darker, and I wondered how he could

still see to make notes in the *Journal*, which has such small type. I switched on the lamp on the sideboard and opened my rucksack to get my things out.

"Because I'm sure that the books by Alexandre Dumas's son wouldn't be as accomplished or as informative. By the way, what did he write?"

"I can't remember. Something called *The Lady of the Camellias*, I think, which is a charming story about a woman and some flowers, who's in love but also very poorly."

I watched Dad as he settled back into the *Journal for Collectors and the Curious*, a little magazine of classified ads that he published himself and that allowed all kinds of collectors to get in touch with each other. But what I really admired about Dad was that he used his little magazine to flag up, to some of these antique lovers, stuff that might interest them. He owned a warehouse in Paris, in which he kept all sorts of old objects waiting to be delivered. He'd taken it over from my grandfather, and it was called "El Dorado". In my imagination it had the mythical allure of a legendary country. I'd never set foot in it, and I didn't even know why Dad called it '"El Dorado". But what I did know was that the day I first went there would be the beginning of a new chapter in my life.

"Dad?"

He looked up from his magazine. He had beautiful blue eyes that glistened a little and it always made me wonder whether he was on the verge of tears.

"Yes?"

"Your father, was he like you are with me? Did he keep an eye on your progress at school?"

Looking at me with his eyes full of emotion, he put the lid back on his pen and waved it in the air, as if he was drawing a long strand of spaghetti.

"He arrived here in France from Poland just before the war, and once peace returned he started selling scrap metal... When that began to take off, he became far too busy with El Dorado to take much notice of how I was doing..."

"So you did super well all on your own?"

He nodded, sucking in his breath, and I was overwhelmed with admiration.

"Dad, tell me, did you love your father a lot?"

He smiled in an awkward sort of way, because some things are difficult to talk about, and took the lid off his pen. I felt he might slip away from me, like a fish from a hook.

"I don't know if I really knew him... And now, when I think about it, I wonder if he even existed.

Do you think it's possible for fathers and sons to know each other?" He looked really serious. The atmosphere was very solemn, as though philosophical storm clouds were gathering.

"Yes, Dad. After all, we know each other, don't we? And my friend Haisam, he knows his father as well as he knows his chessboard..."

Dad considered this for a few seconds. His thoughts seemed to be travelling way back in time.

"Yes, you're right, we know each other, you and I, we do."

He didn't look all that convinced.

"I've got two more questions, but they're not so important."

"Go on then."

"OK, well, to start with, I can't help wondering how teachers can buy their toilet paper in public, in front of other people..."

"I asked myself the same thing at your age. I still don't know the answer. What's the other question?"

"What are we eating tonight?"

"Frogs' legs."

3

I was full of admiration for the way my Egyptian friend and his Turkish father had managed to memorize an impressive number of historically important chess matches. Very late in the evening, or very early in the morning, they could choose to replay the 1973 Bagirov–Gufeld match, or the games that set Reshevsky (who was my dear friend Haisam's favourite player) against Averbakh in 1953, or against Bobby Fischer in 1961. In this way, Haisam travelled through time and circled the world over and over again, without ever leaving those sixty-four black and white squares. He would give me a running commentary, as if I was able to make head or tail of this complicated game, which he calls the game of kings and the king of games. And I was anxious to show that it was worth his while.

"You see," he would explain to me quietly, "Reshevsky gave nothing away. And he had a completely unpredictable style. He wasn't interested in seeking harmony or clarity: he loved to play weird-looking moves that completely destabilized his opponents!"

"I see…"

"That's right! He was also very fond of the Nimzovich Defence as a way to avoid doubled pawns…"

I tried to look as though I understood and was just as much of an expert on the subject as he was.

"Do you see roughly what I mean?" asked Haisam.

"Well, of course I do!"

My friend's eyes were smiling behind his huge spectacles.

Obviously, he must have been pretending to believe I could understand such a complicated game – even more complicated than equations, and they're bad enough – and that was very kind of him.

He pointed towards his father, who had just made a move. "You see," he said, "Averbakh was criticized for that move because the knight is now positioned on g3. He would have been better off playing 8 … c5."

"Just what I was thinking…"

Once I asked him what the point was of rehashing

games that had already been played, since everyone knew the end result.

"It's like revising multiplication tables…"

"Are you saying that for my benefit, to encourage me?"

"Of course not, it was just a comparison…"

"Your player there, what's he called?"

"Reshevsky?"

"Yes, well, I bet he didn't have any problems with multiplication tables or with equations containing variables…"

"I should think not. When he was six he was already playing simultaneous games with twenty adults. He was known as the Escape Artist because his survival instinct got him out of completely desperate situations."

"He was an expert … like Alexandre Dumas."

He smiled and I wondered whether I'd said something stupid.

"Sort of. But what your Alexandre Dumas liked best was stuffing his face and running after women!"

I didn't dare to contradict him, because I didn't have the facts, but I promised myself I'd check up on it anyway.

"And writing too, though," I said, in his defence.

"Yes, of course, writing too. But not as much."

"Well, you have to admit it's a lot less fun!"

We were lined up along the wall outside the maths classroom, waiting for people to come out from the last lesson. I looked around for Marie but all I could see was her mop of curly hair going past, and I noticed that she was quite a lot taller than me. She was very well turned-out, with neat clear lines and nothing slipping over into the margins. I thought about what Dad often said to encourage me to take pride in my appearance: it's the feet that reveal proper care and true refinement. I looked down and saw that Marie's socks were indeed impeccable: ultra white and without a wrinkle, all the way up to her knees.

I felt all blurry in comparison, as though I was about to dissolve.

In class, the teacher handed us a paper with some geometric shapes and questions on it and I realized straight away that it was difficult. I'd spent the previous evening poring over the Krebs manual and various journals to get to the bottom of Dad's question about innovations in the 1901 Paris–Berlin motor race. But I'd fallen asleep without finding the answer, and to cap it all I'd forgotten to do my homework. So I began by sharpening my pencil to get me in the right frame of mind and then I read the first question:

Construct an isosceles triangle ABC with base BC. If E is the reflection of A in the line BC and if T is the translation that maps B to A, prove that the image of E after translation is C.

Checkmate, no doubt about it. I thought about the chess player Reshevsky, who my respectable Egyptian had been talking about. It would have been good to be an Escape Artist like him, with an instinct for survival that would have enabled me to triumph over triangles of any sort; but sadly that wasn't the case. To kill time I dropped my metal ruler, which irritated more or less everyone, including our disabled teacher.

"Victor! I'm going to move you… Take your things and go and sit … over there, next to Marie. At least there I can be sure you won't get distracted."

As I was settling my things on the desk next to Marie, I wanted to smile at her, but her eyes were glued to her worksheet, which was covered with tidy, regular writing, as neat and well-behaved as her socks. For myself, I thought it would be better not to look at either my writing or my socks, because both were shapeless and full of holes. Then I must have gone into a trance, because when I looked down again I found some rough paper in front of me. This is what was on it:

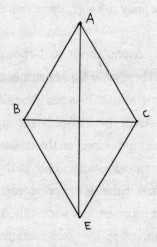

ABC is an isosceles triangle with base BC, therefore AB = AC. E is the reflection of A in the line BC. Therefore AC = EC and AB = EB. EC = AC = AB = EB. ABEC is a rhombus and therefore also a parallelogram. Therefore the image of E after translation is C.

Now here was something that had never happened to me before. I looked around to try and work out who might have had such a kind thought, but nobody caught my eye. It certainly couldn't have been Haisam, sitting at the back of the class. He'd taken off his big glasses and was gazing at some distant horizon. He looked like an enormous bird that had fallen out of its nest: there was something both fragile and indestructible about him. So then I stopped puzzling over it, because I could do that later, and carefully copied out the answer.

During the break I wanted to ask Marie if she was responsible for the miracle. But I couldn't find her; she wasn't the type of girl to hang around in the toilets like the others. I went upstairs to the library. This was more her kind of thing, although I hadn't really spent any time in there myself yet. On TV once, I'd heard this sort of place called a "temple of culture". I preferred to keep my distance, on account of the temple and also the culture.

She wasn't there either. To justify my presence I opened a big dictionary and looked at a random page.

Camellia name given by the botanist Linné in honour of his father Camelli to a shrub with oval, shiny, everlasting leaves and large flowers. The Lady of the Camellias, novel by Alexandre Dumas the younger.

I was glad to find this out. Alexandre Dumas, the son, must have chosen this flower to honour his own father, who'd put so much effort into writing *The Three Musketeers* – a novel so educational that it's been made into films. He wasn't an ungrateful son. I promised myself I'd tell Dad. And it did prove something actually: important things can sometimes take place between father and son. When I put down the dictionary I realized that Marie was there, returning a book to the librarian. I waited for her to leave and then I followed her. I wanted to catch up with her, but the snotty, stuck-up girls were waiting for her, so I was stopped in my tracks.

We spent the last lesson of the day dissecting bulls' eyes, in pairs: Haisam wielded the scalpel and I took notes. I tried to catch Marie's eye, but without success: she was keeping her eyes down while she cut up her eye, if you see what I mean. Then Monsieur Dubois drew some diagrams to show us how a bull sees, and I remember he explained it by drawing a little train in front of the bull. Our eyes worked in the same way, he said. At one point Marie asked a very detailed question, which I didn't entirely catch, because of the complicated words. Monsieur Dubois seemed very surprised so Marie explained.

"It's because my father's a doctor, so sometimes…"

At the end of the lesson I made a show of hanging around in the corridors, so that she could leave first and I could tag along behind. Then I saw Lucky Luke. I thought that was going to spell disaster, because he was heading towards me, and normally that wasn't a good sign. I racked my brains to think what I might have done, but even I couldn't think of anything. My conscience was clear. But had someone told him about the geometric miracle? Did he suspect something?

"How's it going, Victor?"

His manner was friendly, which reassured me a little, but at the same time he seemed to be fretting about something.

"Good, thanks. How about you? You were unlucky in the race last Sunday … loose gravel on the descent always makes things tricky!"

"There's something I want to ask you," he said.

"Yes?"

"Tell me, your *Three Musketeers*, was it Alexandre Dumas the father or the son who wrote it?"

He crossed his arms and looked at me as though he was expecting something important to be solemnly revealed.

"The father, of course. The son mostly wrote stories about poorly flowers."

"Oh, right … what a strange family."

"Why are you asking me?"

"Because reading needs space to breathe."

I thought about how my Honourable Egyptian expressed himself in a symbolic way that you couldn't always understand immediately. Perhaps it was slightly contagious.

"So are you in a bit of a fog about language too then?" I asked him.

"That's enough … you wouldn't understand. Anyway you shouldn't be hanging around in the corridors."

I shot off, because I didn't want things to turn sour. In my experience fraternizing with the authorities rarely makes for a happy life.

Outside, I looked around for Marie and saw her disappearing into the distance. She was on her own, which was unusual, and if I wanted to make the most of it I'd have to get a move on.

I stopped running when I was twenty metres behind her. She'd turned around because I was puffing like a beached whale. Her curly hair was flying all around her face – the wind had got up and the sky seemed to be darkening.

"Do you live in the village too?" she asked as I walked towards her.

"At the edge of it, just after the garage. I don't often see you without your friends. You seem to get on well with them?"

"I see them mainly at school, not so much outside ... I find that they're..."

"—snotty and stuck-up?"

I put my hand in front of my mouth, because of course I realized I'd just said something impolite. I blushed too, which surprised me. I had an urge to run away as fast as my legs would carry me, but I was still too puffed out. All the same, she smiled, though it was a very small smile. She seemed to be considering how to reply.

"I certainly wouldn't have used those words, but I suppose it comes to much the same thing."

We went on for a bit without talking, passing the big houses at the beginning of the village. Suddenly, I burst out.

"By the way, thank you for giving me the answer to the question about the triangle, the iso... iso..."

"—celes?"

"Yes, celes."

"There's nothing to thank me for, because I had nothing to do with it. I didn't even know you'd cheated…"

We were just walking past the church and to be honest I had no idea how to get myself out of this jam, so I said, "Well, in that case there's no other answer: it must have been a miracle. And one should always go and give thanks to God when there's a miracle. It's not the kind of thing I usually do, but still."

I hurtled like a cannonball into the church and knelt down to pray. I mumbled a prayer of my own invention to the patron saint of geometry and triangles, isosceles or whatever. Marie's silhouette was framed in the door like an apparition from ancient times. In the empty church my words sounded like water draining away from a washbasin.

Back outside I attempted to give an impression of dignity, worthy of my dramatic gesture.

"You're weirder than I thought you were," she said thoughtfully, smiling at me in a funny way that might have been a bit sarcastic or a bit sad, or both. She stopped suddenly and pointed at a door in a high stone wall.

"This is where I live."

"Hmm, that's odd…"

"What's odd?"

"Well, your father ... he's a doctor, but there's no brass nameplate..."

"For a start, not all doctors put up a nameplate – for example, those who work in hospitals... And secondly my father isn't a doctor."

"So why did you lie to Monsieur Dubois?"

"Do I ask you why you blocked the girls' toilets, just after lunch, with the loo paper you hide under the washbasins? We had stomach pains all afternoon!"

I ignored that and said, "So then it wasn't you who gave me the answer to the question? Are you sure?"

"Of course I'm sure. Why do you think I would do something like that?"

She opened the door with a big key and I just had time to glimpse a huge garden, almost the size of a park. She was about to disappear, but then she turned around and said, "If you want, you can come and do your homework with me one day."

I was flattered, but the word "homework" bothered me a bit.

That evening, I left Dad by himself to muddle through with his research in his magazine, the *Journal for*

Collectors and the Curious. He was a bit surprised, because usually on Friday evenings I liked to help him take notes in it, sorting out his orders and deliveries. I told him I needed to think things over. I knew it was an activity he took seriously and even encouraged. We agreed to get together the next morning and take the Panhard out for a spin.

When I got to my room, the first thing I did was to open the dictionary:

Miracle *from the Latin* miraculum, *"a wonder", from* mirari, *"to wonder at". An extraordinary event believed to result from a benign divine intervention and to which a spiritual significance is attached.*

I thought the dictionary went a bit over the top about the word "miracle", but on the whole I agreed. In any event I wasn't a particular expert in divine matters. I took all my books out from my desk, even the ones from last year, because it couldn't do any harm. I came across a little manual given to me by a lady that my father had taken me to see, because of my difficulties. My visits to her didn't last long, because a month after our first meeting she moved away and we never saw her again. Dad said it couldn't have been anything to do with me,

60

she must have been planning it already.

At the beginning of this little book, the writers, who were specialists in other people's difficulties, had included a sort of quiz so that kids like me could see how they were doing. It was very kind of them, like a mark of confidence. I spent part of the evening answering the questions, which were set out a bit like a game. When you'd finished, you had to see where you were in the following categories, according to the marks you'd got:

15/20 to 20/20: *You have understood the lesson well. Well done! Go straight to the exercises.*

8/20 to 14/20: *You have some difficulties. Check your mistakes and review those parts of the lesson and the sample exercises that you didn't understand.*

0/20 to 7/20: *You have serious difficulties. Study the lesson in depth and do all the sample exercises.*

So, I had *serious* difficulties. I had to study the lesson in *depth* and do *all* the sample exercises. It doesn't take long for assessments to become disheartening. I flicked through the little booklet's contents. There were questions about cosines, distances between points, translations, cones, proportionality and a lot of other things with names I won't mention. I threw the booklet across the room and it smashed against my electric guitar like a pancake.

How could I ever begin to make progress? I felt as though I was in a rowing boat that was leaking everywhere, without enough fingers to plug the holes. I couldn't even manage to find the answer to the 1901 Paris–Berlin innovations question. I thought about the chess player Reshevsky again. Haisam had told me that he was legendary because he grew up without a coach or any training method, but overcame this disadvantage because of his natural talent. I didn't have any training method or coach, but nor did I have any natural talent to help me overcome my disadvantages. I was certainly no Escape Artist! Only a miracle could save me. I wondered what I would do if Marie invited me to go and do my homework at her place. It was different with Haisam. I'd made a fool of myself in front of him a few times, but it didn't count, because he had a noble soul. He never passed judgement and he was always helpful. Since I'd told him the maths teacher carried her dead baby in her right leg, and it was probably the weight of it that made her limp, he'd taken me really seriously. But was Marie as good at understanding people as my Honourable Egyptian was?

"The truth is, I'm not up to it," I said to my father, who was jabbing at the Panhard's gear lever.

Very early the next morning, we'd taken the main road heading south. We'd left the scattered outskirts behind us and now we were driving alongside a large forest. The trees were reaching their great bare arms up into the empty sky, which looked really awesome in the still morning. I'd taken the Krebs manual with me, as well as a notebook we kept specifically for anything to do with the Panhard.

"Up to what?" asked my father.

"Up to things in general. They make it quite clear in that little book that Madame Picques gave me last year. You remember – that very nice lady who moved away after meeting me. She told me to do the tests. And it's obvious that I'm not up to it. They put it very nicely in the book, they make an effort not to be discouraging, they respect the pride and dignity of dimwits like me. But all the same it's their kindness that makes you feel like an idiot … and in the end I've just got to get used to the idea that I'm never going to get out of this mess. Unless there's a miracle…"

"A what?"

He was frowning as if he didn't really understand, or as if I was speaking a foreign language.

"A miracle. A divine intervention, if you like."

"Perhaps you just need a bit longer than other people. If you get discouraged straight away because you're lagging behind the pack... You'll find a way to get closer to the front of the race..."

"This is nothing to do with sport! Did you know that the chess player Reshevsky, when he was six years old, played games against twenty adults at the same time and won them all? And he didn't even have a coach..."

"So?"

"So I don't even know how to play dominoes."

"You never learned..."

"That's exactly the problem... Remember when Uncle Zak tried to teach me chess and I couldn't even recognize the knight? And this summer Haisam tried to teach me the basics too, but they won't go in... The thing's got too many diagonals for me... And that stupid old horse moves in a really shifty way."

"Lots of people don't know how to play chess..."

"But it's like that with everything: cosines, cones, the climate of the South of France. Even spelling:

today I wrote "predidgious" instead of "prodigious". I'm telling you, something's not right."

Just then we drove through a little village of houses built in stone. We passed some farms that still hadn't woken up, with big signs outside saying TURNIPS.

"Look at that," said Dad. "They're insulting us!"

I started to smile and then it bubbled up inside me and I burst out laughing and so did Dad and we couldn't stop. The Panhard was zigzagging all over the place, in that crystal-clear morning light. Suddenly, whole flocks of brightly coloured cyclists overtook us, swaying on their saddles and sweating from the pain in their buttocks. Dad wound down the window:

"Slackers!" he yelled. "Capitalists!"

And he put his foot down hard on the accelerator, making sparks fly out of the old car. It was a grand comic gesture, even if I didn't completely understand the term "capitalist". I just assumed it meant something similar to "slacker". Then Dad turned on the car stereo and we listened to "Satisfaction" by the Rolling Stones: rock music at its very finest. It was funny to hear Dad trying to sing like Mick Jagger.

The Panhard ground to a halt in a little village. We got out and went to sit in a café. I admired the firm way that Dad shook the owner's hand: he must have been one of his clients because Dad told him that the "goods" hadn't arrived yet. I didn't know what goods he was talking about, but the term didn't surprise me much, because Dad used it a lot when he was talking on the telephone to his clients. I asked for some hot chocolate and a sandwich and looked at the notebook. I should have taken more notice of how the Panhard was running, because the whole point of being out on the road at dawn was to make sure everything was working smoothly. If you give the Panhard its head for two minutes it starts to go on the blink. It's a thoroughbred car, renowned for its sensitivity, and there's always some minor thing wrong with it. Its Achilles heel is its exhaust system.

My father came back from the counter holding a plate.

"My feeling," he said, "is that the valves are making a funny noise."

"A sort of clicking?"

"Yes."

"I'll make a note."

I took a sip of chocolate and flicked through the Krebs manual.

"In my opinion," he said, "we need to take out the cylinder."

"You just need to be careful there isn't too much play in the valve rocker arms. Because you know what happened last time…"

"Hey, you've got a moustache!"

He was smiling. I wiped my sleeve across my mouth to shave off the moustache. And then I smiled too.

"You see, Dad, the problem is that I'm all blurry."

"Blurry?"

"That's what I was thinking the other day, when the maths teacher sat me next to one of the girls in the class."

He was smiling again.

"And so she was less blurry than you?"

"She wasn't at all blurry. Quite the opposite, she was very clearly defined. She'd be an instant cure for any short-sighted person who looked at her. And do you know what it was that got me thinking like this?"

"No."

"Well, it was her socks."

Neither of us said anything for a few seconds. Then I went on.

"Dad…?"

"Yes?"

"You need to buy me some new socks, with good elastic, that pull up straight. I truly believe I'll do better at school with the right kind of socks – supercharged socks in fact! But hey, Dad, at my age did you dress smartly?"

He thought for a bit. Some hikers came into the café.

"Very smartly. I used to wear a tie and a waistcoat. And loafers."

My father thought that looking smart was a sort of passport, and that if my grandfather – who'd handed down his taste for elegance – hadn't been dressed like a duke, he'd never have managed to fit in when he arrived in France.

I tried to imagine him smartly dressed in the playground, and it made me feel a bit emotional, because of the way that the past is almost as unreachable as the future.

"So, your miracle, will it be the socks?"

"In a way."

We went back to the Panhard and got her going

again. Dad manoeuvred the gear lever very gently, almost stroking it.

Then he put the Rolling Stones back on.

4

By the end of the following school week I'd come to accept that Marie had nothing to do with the mathematical miracle. I even began to think I might have written down the answer myself without realizing it. History tells of even stranger things than that happening – I can't think of any examples right now – but I know it's a thought that came to me at the time.

On the day the teacher handed back our papers, all my doubts disappeared and everything became clear, because Marie had a lower mark than me. And that was out of the question: it was scientifically impossible, with or without divine intervention. A big deal was made of congratulating me and I even felt quite choked: it was very touching. In the end I took the praise seriously, as though I'd actually deserved it, with all the stress that went with it. The whole class was looking at me and I was struck that no one seemed to suspect anything. Even Haisam had roused himself so as not to miss this important moment. A very sweet smile was spreading across his great face, which radiated calm and trust. My heart was beating double fast from the emotion. The teacher kept on and on: it was turning into a real awards ceremony, as though I'd won some geometrical Oscar. I thought she was going a bit over the top, but it was good to stack up some praise, since it was a long time since I'd had any. She even compared me to Marie when she gave her back her work. It was the first time I'd ever heard the teacher trying out a bit of humour.

"You see, you did even better than Marie, who made a big error right at the end. That's how I know you didn't copy her work!"

But then things began to go wrong, because after the lesson the teacher came limping up to me and said, "No more excuses now! You've proved that you can do perfectly well if you put a bit of effort into it. So I'm counting on you, OK?"

She looked me straight in the eyes. And then she added solemnly, as if she was presiding over some age-old ceremony, "*Everyone's* counting on you!"

I got out of there with the feeling that I was balancing the fate of the world on the end of my pen, and all I could think was that I was completely screwed. It would have been good to talk to Marie, but she'd dashed off and disappeared. As I walked down the corridor, I felt like I'd just been in a boxing match. I looked out for Etienne and Marcel, who were the other two members of the rock band I'd founded, but they must have been out in the playground already, kicking their ball around.

Downstairs, trying to sneak as quietly as possible past his office, I bumped into Lucky Luke and that was the final straw, because he started banging on about it as well.

"Good sprint, young man, an excellent breakaway, as they say in the Tour de France! I've heard about your achievements. It's the yellow jersey for you! Bravo! Worthy of a musketeer!"

He put a hand on my shoulder, as though he was really proud of me.

"I hope you're pleased!"

"Yes, sir, very pleased…"

"I knew we could count on you and that all our educational efforts weren't in vain."

He gave me the thumbs-up.

It was too much to bear. I ran to the toilets, because I felt completely overcome and didn't want to show myself up in front of everyone. I had my dignity to think of. Shutting myself myself in one of the cubicles (there were always plenty free since I'd been hiding the toilet paper) I burst into tears. I felt much better after that.

I decided to think things over a bit, right there on the toilet. I'd often dreamed of receiving such a torrent of compliments, but it was a bit like getting a Christmas present that was far too expensive. Now it had actually happened I was in shock. But it wasn't only a question of my emotions. I also had to address the problem the situation had created: now I was saddled with a responsibility. Before, I didn't need to measure up to anything at all, and that was quite relaxing, whereas now the whole world was expecting results from me. There was a risk of upsetting everyone, and frankly it's really stressful when you're weighed down with other people's disappointment, because it doesn't leave much room for hope. I wanted to admit defeat, go find Lucky Luke and tell him the whole story: that it was a scam, that I'd cheated disgracefully and that he could expect nothing from me. My career as a good pupil was getting off to a really bad start, with nothing but worry and regret. I flushed the toilet, wondering why everything I had anything to do with always ended in confusion.

In the playground, I spotted Etienne and Marcel. They were both playing right wing, because they were both left-footed. They were brothers, and I'd started calling them "the Metro" when I learned that there's a Metro station in Paris called "Etienne Marcel". They played bass guitar and drum extremely badly but I wasn't very picky about performance quality and I'd allowed them to join the band. To celebrate the band's birth, we'd cracked a bottle of apple juice over the old electric guitar that Dad had bought me. He'd suggested a brilliant name for us, "The Rattletraps". What's more he'd also given us permission to practise in the workshop at the back of the yard. I don't know what gave him the idea of the name "The Rattletraps", and I did wonder whether it was much of a compliment to our performances, but anyway... One day we'd given our music teacher a demo of our best pieces. He appreciated our efforts, but he said there was a technical problem, because all he could hear was metal being hit and whooshing sounds.

"It's odd," he said, a little awkwardly, "it sounds

74

like you recorded it in … a blacksmith's forge … or … on an airport runway!"

We took back the tape and we never forgave him after that, because artists are sensitive.

Just before the bell rang, I asked Etienne and Marcel what they thought about my predicament. Obviously, I avoided telling them that Marie was undoubtedly behind the whole thing, because I already felt enough of a fool. Etienne suggested that I should actually become the Escape Artist that the Honourable Egyptian had talked about and continue to cheat to maintain the high standard I'd reached.

"That's impossible, I'm too dumb to cheat properly. I tried last year and it was a total failure. I got a detention and I had to clean all the school toilets. So no thanks. And anyway I've got principles. Haven't you?"

"No."

Marcel raised his eyes to the sky and recommended quite simply that I work hard enough to succeed honestly. Of course, when I was thinking things over on the toilet, I'd also considered this option.

"I'm too far behind. However hard I try, I just get into a complete muddle. For example, this morning's biology lesson with those wrinkled peas and smooth peas that show whatever it is they show – if I go over it again this evening, I'm sure I won't understand a thing!"

"All great rock musicians are famous for having disastrous school careers," said Etienne, pompously.

There was a long respectful silence.

"And you *are* a great rock musician," he added as an afterthought.

After school, I warned Haisam that I wouldn't be coming to watch them play chess, because there was something more urgent I needed to do.

"That's a shame," he said, "because I was planning to introduce you to the secrets of the Sicilian Defence."

It was obvious that the whole school was now conspiring to make a fool of me but I pretended not to notice. "Maybe tomorrow," I suggested.

"Impossible. Tomorrow's Saturday."

"So?"

"So it's the Sabbath. And on the Sabbath you're not allowed to do anything."

"But you're an Egyptian, an Honourable Egyptian. And your father's a Turk, a Turk from Istanbul."

"From Galata, actually. And anyway what's that got to do with it?"

I couldn't think of a satisfactory answer, and in any case my mind was on other things. Haisam opened the door to the lodge. Inside, his father, wearing his fez, was kneading bread. Before shutting the door on me, my Honourable Egyptian said, "I have the feeling that your haste to leave school has something to do with your triumph today." He looked at me with his X-ray eyes. I felt sure he could see through to my skeleton.

"What if it has?" I replied, just like that, without thinking.

He nodded slowly, as if to say it was a good answer, and it sent shivers down my spine, because he made me feel taller.

I ran all the way to the village to be sure I wouldn't miss her. I didn't have the patience to wait all weekend to get this thing sorted. I felt like going back into the church to pray that she would be on her own, but twice in such a short space of time would undoubtedly have looked suspect, up there on high, where they can be touchy about etiquette. I crossed my fingers instead. When she appeared, on her own, with her foamy mop of hair, I practically threw myself at her. She jumped, startled.

"Hey, you frightened me. Are you OK?"

"No."

"Oh, why's that? You've had a good day, what with all the compliments you got."

"That's just the trouble."

"What on earth's the matter with you? Explain yourself."

I felt irritation creeping over me, but I was anxious to rein it in, because there was nothing to stop her dumping me right there and heading straight home. Also, it was important to explain the situation with precision and clarity – two essential qualities you need to have in life, so Dad had told me. I noticed she'd taken off her big ring.

"Don't pretend you don't understand. You know exactly what kind of a mess I'm in."

She sat down on the bench in front of the church.

"Tell me then, but make it quick. Because I've got to go home."

"All right, well then, today I got a better mark than you…"

"Yes, I made a mistake in the last step."

"Don't give me that… Everyone's ganging up on me today… I know perfectly well that it was you who gave me the answer and that you made a mistake on purpose to cover it up…"

78

I crossed my arms to show I was serious, and then I crossed my legs too because I was in a panic.

"Why would I have done that? But let's say I did. What's the problem, since you got the highest mark in the class?"

I searched for words that would match the strength of my feeling. My eyes were drawn to the church's weathervane, which kept changing direction. I was just thinking that meant a storm was on the way when all of a sudden Marie stood up. I followed close on her heels and trotted along behind her.

"Everyone knows I've turned over a new leaf. I'm the only one, except for you, who knows I didn't do it on my own and that it's been a complete con from beginning to end. Even Lucky Luke congratulated me, and I'm sure my father's been told."

"So what's the problem?"

"The problem is that I'm now going to disappoint everyone and I'm really stressed about it. It's hopeless. I'll never be able to do it again. As soon as we get the next test I'll be back to the bottom of the class and I'll be found out…"

"Unless…"

"Unless nothing. I'm going to stop you right there. Whatever you do, don't suggest I cheat again… And by the way, that shows it was you who—"

"Let's say. But I wasn't going to suggest…"

She slowed down and I realized we'd got to her place. But there was no way I was going to let her slip through my fingers like that. I stood in front of the door to her house and crossed my arms again.

"So let's be clear about this: was it or wasn't it you?"

Her curly hair hid her face while she calmly looked for the keys in her bag.

"OK. It was me."

Oddly, I couldn't think of anything else to say. She was smiling at me, with her lips pressed together.

"And why did you do that? You see what you've got me into? It's like starving people in Africa: if you give them a feast straight away, well, they croak pretty much pronto. It would have been better to take it more slowly with me as well."

"I didn't think of that. It's not really my thing – cheating, I mean… Not thinking isn't really my thing either."

For a few seconds I thought about whether I ought to find this a good enough excuse or not. My head was pounding, as though an army was marching through it in formation.

"I've got to go home to practise my cello … but if you want you can come and listen to me."

I almost said that I was a musician too, but I held back. I was curious to see her cello. Dad would be worried. Then I'd be worried about him being worried, and it was a pain when we were both worrying about each other. But I followed Marie anyway. We walked through the big garden on a gravel path that weaved between a great many trees of all different varieties. At one point she whispered to me, "By the way, thank you for putting the loo paper back in the girls' toilets."

I thought it all over later that evening. I had a splitting headache and Dad didn't think I looked too good. I just about had the energy to take my temperature and head off to bed. When Dad asked what had got me into such a state I simply replied, "I was given too much to digest in one go."

Since this didn't mean much to him, I added, "I got the best mark in the class."

He knew that anyway, because he'd bumped into Lucky Luke out training on his bike and they'd discussed my case together, agreeing that all was not lost.

In any event, he seemed to find it odd that I

was torturing myself about a good mark; but there were things he needed to do with the Panhard, so he stomped off, saying that I was never satisfied and that complicating everything wouldn't bring me happiness. But then I hadn't given him the full story.

I thought again about the time I'd spent at Marie's house. I'd got lumbered with an hour and a half of cello with Vivaldi, Bach and a composer called Marin something, who I'd never heard of.

At last she'd put down her bow and asked, "Do you like music too?"

"Yes," I said.

"Classical or baroque?"

"Baraque? What's baraque?"

"Baroque. Not baraque."

I blushed bright red because of my old enemy, ignorance. I didn't know the difference, but baroque meant absolutely nothing to me and I even wondered whether it was some kind of a trap. Classical seemed to me to be more ... classical.

"Classical. Because the other one, well..."

"Who's your favourite composer?"

My brain started whizzing. It wasn't the moment to try and be clever. I don't know why, but I thought about the food we used to give to my rabbit that died last year. It was called "Mozart Mix".

"Mozart. My favourite's Mozart."

I smiled broadly with relief. I could look him up later.

"Any particular piece?"

"Oh … pretty much all of them. I'm a big fan."

She went back to rubbing her bow with some weird stuff that looked like wax.

"What's that?" I asked, trying to show some interest.

"It's rosin. It makes the bow grip the strings better."

It looked as though she was giving the bow a long, slow stroke.

I stood up because I had pins and needles in my legs. I looked at all the books, lined up alphabetically in the bookcase. I noticed immediately that there were a lot of books about eyes, which was strange: *Anatomy of the Optic Nerve, Pathology of the Human Eye, Learning about Blindness*, and so on. And others with titles so complicated that they might as well have been books about wizardry.

"That's strange," I said, "all these books about eyes. How come you're interested in that?"

"It's for my project."

"What project?"

"You know, I suggested to the form teacher that I should give a presentation to the class about Helen Keller's life story, based on the book she wrote."

"So, what's that got to do with eyes?"

"Well, Helen Keller was an American girl who lost her sight when she was eighteen months old. She became very knowledgeable and very well-known, thanks to her teacher who did everything she could to help her... That's what it's about – in a nutshell – obviously. If you want, I could lend you the book."

"No thanks, I've got enough to do with *The Three Musketeers*. Later, perhaps, when I've finished it ... in ten years' time. By the way, something that's been bothering me... Do you know if it's true that Alexandre Dumas was mostly interested in, you know, stuffing his face and chasing girls?"

"I think it is true."

I was a bit disappointed. I'd rather hoped that Haisam was wrong. But the Honourable Egyptian is never wrong.

"So you need all these books for your presentation?"

"I like to have all the facts when I take on a task."

"Mind you, it's not surprising you're interested in eyes and blind people…"

"Why do you say that?"

"Because a lot of blind people are also very talented musicians. You've got something in common with them."

She said nothing and her face clouded right over. I had the impression I'd made a real blunder. Although to be honest that's not an unusual feeling for me.

The house was quiet, and occasionally you could hear the wood creaking.

"Are you all on your own here? Where are your parents?"

"They'll come home later. I'm often on my own. My parents are art experts and auctioneers, so they go away a lot."

"What are auction ears?"

"You know: going … going … gone!"

She hit the table with an invisible hammer. I'd seen that in films.

Neither of us said anything for a few minutes. I needed to find a topic of conversation quickly. I immediately dismissed anything to do with music, because the truth is, I wasn't up to it. And that made me think I should tell the Metro to keep shtum about our own lousy musical performances. Of course, the more I tried to think of something to say, the harder it was to come up with anything. In the end I felt it would be best to leave, because it was going to get awkward. She put away her cello, sat down on her bed and stared hard at me.

"I've got something I want to put to you…"

I felt my head shrink down into my shoulders. I smelt a rat.

"Yes, what?"

"Well, look. I've got you into a mess by trying to help you…"

"Yes, but it's my fault as well. I'm too complicated to take this sort of thing lightly."

"You know I'm a good student."

"Everyone knows that."

"My parents had me tested. I remember the result. The psychologist's words are engraved on my brain: 'Very high IQ.'"

"IQ? What does that stand for? Incredible quality?"

"Intelligence quotient, you dummy. You know, what you have in your brain… And mine is well above average, with an astonishing memory and an exceptional aptitude for conceptualization."

I tried to look as though I understood, but I didn't

know what the word "conceptualization" meant. I wasn't too sure about "aptitude" either.

"So what?" I said. "I couldn't care less. Do you want to give me your CV as well?"

"I couldn't care less either, that's not the point. The point is that if you want, I can help you study."

"Study?"

"Yes. Revise with you. Explain things you haven't understood. Help you catch up."

My mouth dropped open and all the colours of the rainbow must have passed across my face. My brain was completely scrambled and everything was getting jumbled up: Reshevsky, Alexandre Dumas, Mozart, Marin what's-his-name, the lady with the Camellias and d'Artagnan, even Lucky Luke and the Tour de France. I barely had the strength to reply.

"I'll have to think about it. I need to get used to the idea."

To be honest, it didn't really tie in with how I thought of myself: as a kind of subversive guitar hero.

I picked up my coat, but just before leaving I asked her, as a sort of challenge, "What if I asked you to name the technical innovation that was introduced in Panhard cars in the 1901 Paris–Berlin motor race?

Hmm? Would you be able to find that out?"

"I'll find it out."

That's it, you have a good look, brainbox, I said to myself on the way home, savouring my victory in advance. *Look as hard as you like...*

5

Subject	Average Mark	General Comments
French	4.5	THERE HAS BEEN PROGRESS IN RECENT WEEKS. HOWEVER, I WOULD LIKE TO REMIND VICTOR THAT THE FRENCH WRITER GUSTAVE FLAUBERT ISN'T A JOURNALIST AND THAT THE RUSSIAN AUTHOR DOSTOYEVSKY DIDN'T WRITE "THE BROTHERS KALASHNIKOV".
Maths	5	A MIRACLE OCCURRED HALFWAY THROUGH THE TERM. NEVERTHELESS, VICTOR IS REQUESTED TO STOP SIGNING HIS WORK "ALBERT EINSTEIN".
History and Geography	4	VICTOR'S WORK IS IMPROVING, BUT I'D LIKE TO KNOW WHAT HE THINKS TOOTIN' CARMEN HAS TO DO WITH A-NCIENT EGYPT.

Biology	5	VICTOR IS MAKING AN EFFORT, BUT I WOULD ASK HIM TO STOP LOOKING FOR TRANSPARENT FOSSILS, WHICH SEEM TO HAVE BECOME AN OBSESSION WITH HIM. MY FROGS HAVE HAD NO CAUSE FOR COMPLAINT THIS YEAR. AT LEAST, THOSE THAT SURVIVED THE GENOCIDE.
PE and Sport	2.5	I know you hidε bεhind thε planε trεεs during long-distancε running: I can sεε your bεaniε hat poking out!
Music	6	Victor has been drawing cellos on his desk, which indicates a new direction in his musical tastes. But he still sings out of tune.

It was the end of term. Dad was reading my report and I was reading over his shoulder, standing on tiptoe. I'd been very curious to know what this one would look like. Since Marie had become my coach, she'd kept my nose pressed so close to the handlebars that I could hardly see where I was going or what I was doing. But the rest of the class were almost in sight and I was pedalling as fast as I could to catch up with them. It reminded me of the time when Dad and I were about to move into the house. We had to redecorate the walls. I spent days slapping whitewash over them, but my face was almost touching the surface so I couldn't see that it was all patchy. It needed another coat.

Still, it was the only report I'd ever had that I wasn't dreading too much. The first thing I did was to find a calculator and work out my average mark, so that I could really get to grips with my performance. Dad had started sniggering under his breath.

"What's so funny? Are you laughing at me?"

"The Brothers Kalashnikov ... really! Aren't you ashamed of yourself?"

He rolled up the report and tried to hit me on the head with it, but I managed to dodge him.

"Ka-ra-ma-zov! Not Kalashnikov!"

He was laughing out loud now, with little tears in the corners of his eyes.

"And Flaubert a journalist! Why not a TV newsreader?"

"It was Uncle Zak who told me that Flaubert worked for the papers."

That made Dad look a little sad.

Thinking about Uncle Zak brought a lump to my throat too. He'd gone off on his travels again, on a journey to the land of our ancestors.

Eventually Dad said, "All things considered, it's not too bad, I admit. Some of the comments are even quite encouraging."

On the whole, I pretty much agreed with him.

"Except for sport, obviously," he added.

The thing is, Marie and I had decided to ignore the issue of sport. We'd thought it best to concentrate on the key priorities.

"But sport's important, you know!"

He pretended to dribble with an invisible ball, which was quite funny.

"Take me, for example, Victor: when I was young, I was the Paris team's top player."

"Are you having me on?"

He mimed shooting the ball into the net as hard as he could.

"Of course I am! But it's still true that sport is important."

There was a moment of silence. Dad gave me back the report and then began to clear away the cups from the living-room table. He started off towards the kitchen and then suddenly turned around.

"Your mum would be proud of you!" he blurted out.

And then off he went. I heard him rummaging around in the cupboards.

"Dad?" I asked, while he was still in the kitchen.

"Yes?"

"Did you love Mum a lot?"

He didn't answer straight away and it felt as though the whole house was swallowed in silence. I held my breath. I heard him coming back towards me and looked up to see his slightly faded blue eyes. I thought to myself, *If one day you're not here any more, Dad, I'm going to keep the blue of your eyes to warm my heart.*

He pretended to be absorbed in his journal. He was like a wounded animal that withdraws from the world, which was an awesome expression I'd heard at school.

"Yes, I loved her very much. Do you remember when she left?"

"Not really. I only remember that around that time Uncle Zak came back from a long trip and lived with us for a while."

"And then it was just the two of us. And without you I'd have been sunk. Do you understand?"

"Yes, Dad, I understand about things in the great pool of life."

It was properly solemn. Dad did a fart to break the tension, and I did a smaller one out of solidarity. And after that we had a good laugh.

* * *

Then I got my rucksack out, with the stuff I was supposed to revise that week. Marie was expecting me that afternoon and later the Metro were supposed to be coming over for a jamming session. I hadn't told them what was going on – because I had my reputation as a subversive guitar hero to think of – but they were beginning to wonder where I disappeared to for whole afternoons at a time. I hadn't said anything to Haisam either, but I think he had his suspicions, because my Honourable Egyptian always had suspicions about everything.

I'd hesitated for a long time before agreeing to Marie's proposal. I thought there might be something fishy about it. I still wasn't entirely sure I could trust her, with her oh-so-white socks, her stratospheric IQ and her cello, which seemed like a living creature that was difficult to tame – while I made do with my old busted guitar and whatever sound I could get out of it. We weren't at all in the same league, Marie and me. I wasn't a match for her and I couldn't see what she could possibly find interesting about me. I often felt like a weird little animal, shrivelled up and insignificant, being studied under a scientist's microscope.

I began to change my mind the day I found this, written on a piece of paper in my pencil case:

In May 1901, Panhard and Levassor were the first company to introduce an engine without a cylinder head gasket, as well as a three-point engine suspension system.

To tell the truth I was totally speechless, because despite trawling through the Krebs manual every evening, I hadn't been able to find that information. That evening I asked Dad and he confirmed it was right, but I refused to tell him where I'd got the answer, because I have my pride.

The next day I was still hesitating and thinking it over when the history teacher asked me, in front of the whole class, "So, Victor, can you tell me what Gutenberg invented?"

I didn't stop to think, which is generally a bad mistake in life.

"The copier!" I answered. That exclamation mark shows how sure of myself I felt and how pleased I was with my answer. Of course everyone burst out laughing, all the more so because it was a while since I'd been held up for ridicule. I'd got out of the habit of it too. I thought the teacher was going to tear a strip off me, but it was even worse than that because she just asked, "Laser or inkjet?"

The first few weeks hadn't been easy. I had to dig out all my old papers, which were scrunched up in balls in the waste bin. I asked Dad for the iron and he was amazed to see me flattening the cosines, smoothing out the three-dimensional diagrams, pressing the graphs and then hanging the papers up on the clothes line in the kitchen.

After that, Marie spent a few days studying my essays, which were all stiff from being ironed. Then she told me the story of two writers that she'd read about in a book. One of them was seventeen and was having trouble writing his novel. The other one was quite a lot older. He was very fond of the younger one, so he shut him in a room in his house with a pile of paper and a bottle of whisky, and told him to slide the pages under the door as he wrote them. When the younger one had written enough, the older one let him out. Later, the younger one died suddenly and the older one said that his grief was so great that it felt like having a limb amputated without anaesthetic. Marie thought this was a very interesting story. Personally, I thought that if he didn't like writing, what was the point of forcing him, and perhaps that's what killed him in the end. Alexandre

Dumas certainly didn't need to be shut in a room to write *The Three Musketeers*. But I kept quiet, because I could see that Marie was trying to draw a parallel with our situation, and I felt a bit flattered by that.

So she settled me down at her desk, on her work chair, with an alarming quantity of exercises and revision to do.

On her way out, she said, "I'm not locking you in and I'm not giving you any whisky, because you should never copy the way things are done in books … but it's the same idea!"

Instead of whisky, I was allowed a glass of pomegranate juice. I could hear her sawing at her cello while I was trying to work. It took me aback, the way she was spending more and more time attacking her instrument. There was a sort of violent rage to it – she was usually so calm and collected. It was as though her life depended upon it. And in fact it did, in a way, although of course I only knew that later.

In the end, I felt as though the lines on my paper were turning into musical staves and I was walking a tightrope along them. After I'd finished my work she told me more about all her favourite composers and as time went on I got to know them really quite well – Johann Sebastian Bach, for instance, who'd been married twice and had twenty children. Marie wondered how he could have written so much music when he had all those children under his feet.

"Well, he certainly made good use of his organ," I couldn't resist saying.

"Very funny. And what's more you know, he had problems with his sight."

"Oh, really? I thought that was Beethoven."

"No, with Beethoven it was his ears. He was as deaf as a post."

"That's less distinguished… Musicians all seem to be disabled, as far as I can see."

"Bach had to have an eye operation. But it didn't work and he went completely blind."

She had gone all thoughtful.

"In those days, it can't have been much fun, going to hospital and having your eyes messed around with," I said.

"No. I expect things have improved since then."

Anyway, as soon as I arrived at her house on the day I got my report, I laid it out in front of her so that she could compare our results. Her hair had grown since the beginning of the school year and while she was reading her face was completely invisible, swamped by its flaming foaminess.

She smiled, parting her lips to expose a row of teeth polished bright like pearls.

"Tootin' Carmen…? Wait… You didn't really, did you? I can't believe it… Do you mean Tutankhamun? I can't think how you come up with these things. One could rack one's brain for weeks without thinking up anything so funny."

"I find it difficult to copy down from the board. I promise you that's what was written in my exercise book. I'd revised Ancient Egypt."

"This we have to celebrate."

We went downstairs to the kitchen. Marie poured the pomegranate juice into a big jug and put it on a tray with a plate of biscuits. Then we went into the sitting room.

"Sit over there on the sofa."

She got the cello out of its case and began to apply rosin to the bow. The vigorous way she rubbed at it reminded me of horse riders I'd seen brushing their horses with handfuls of straw, to stop them catching cold. Maybe the cello was like a delicate animal too. She opened up some sheet music on her stand. It was covered with complicated symbols that marked out time and I wondered how she could possibly get her bearings. Then she put the cello between her knees and began to attack it with her bow as though this time she wanted to smack it or saw it right through. It took me a while to get the rhythm and tune, because it was an awkward kind of music and I wasn't used to it. I couldn't get my head around the deluge of notes. But little by little I felt like I was waking up and I allowed myself to be carried along by the unfamiliar sounds. There was another world to discover... And perhaps, after all, there was something somewhere as beautiful as "Satisfaction" by the Rolling Stones. It was difficult to imagine, but why shouldn't there be?

So the time passed, with Marie stopping occasionally to turn the page or take a sip of pomegranate juice. I noticed that she was very pretty, with her tangled mop of hair swaying to the same rhythm as her bow. It was a kind of beauty that had nothing in common with the other girls at school, who wore their jeans so tight you could almost see what was underneath. I realized that I'd hardly ever thought of her as a girl the same age as me. Perhaps I hadn't even though of her as a girl at all.

When she stopped playing, it was already late and seventeenth-century music was ringing in my ears.

There was so much of it bubbling around inside me that I could hardly stand up.

"It's too late to work now, let's go for a walk in the park. We deserve a day of rest."

The big house was still completely empty and cold, as though it had been abandoned. Once or twice I'd seen a cleaner with a feather duster moving around the rooms. Marie always spoke to her very politely and I must say I thought it showed real class to be so respectful.

As we walked down the gravel path leading to the main road, I asked her, "Aren't your parents ever around?"

"Yes, but they get home late. They're often in London valuing works of art. One of these days I'll ask them to invite you over for lunch."

"OK, but I'll need to swot up."

She smiled.

As we reached the park gates, the sun was setting. I was going to be late for The Rattletraps, but too bad!

"How come you took to playing the cello? It's an unusual thing to do, after all..."

"It started when I was three: I saw a musician rubbing rosin on his bow and it seemed such a gentle, peaceful thing to do that I wanted to stroke the strings too. Obviously, my parents were a bit disappointed that I wasn't particularly interested in painting, but in the end they were just really pleased I'd found something I was passionate about. And I really am passionate about it … I couldn't live without it… It must be the same sort of thing for your friend Haisam, with his chess and his maths."

That stopped me in my tracks. She must have noticed, because she burst out laughing.

"I saw you in the caretaker's lodge! He comes across as really intelligent, your pal Haisam."

"Extremely intelligent," I said, putting on a very serious voice as if I was the one to judge.

I was a bit hurt that she was saying all this about the Honourable Egyptian, even if I did completely agree with her and maybe had a higher opinion of him than she did. Once again I felt like a little nobody by comparison.

"I'm different," I said. "I don't know how to do anything particularly interesting. I'll be reading *The Three Musketeers* until I'm twenty-one and then if I start on *The Lady of the Camellias*, well, I'll still be reading it when I retire. At least that'll save money on books. I'll never be able to learn chess, nor music theory with all its cadavers and semi-cadavers."

"Quavers and semi-quavers!"

"You see... I get my words muddled! Even when it comes to Panhard cars, you're cleverer than me."

We'd walked as far as the pond, where three swans were swimming around. With their straight necks they looked like umbrellas floating upside down. We sat down on a bench. It was quiet there, and we were quiet too. She was sitting bolt upright next to me and I couldn't bring myself to look at her any more. It was clear I was no match for her. We had nothing in common, and I still hadn't worked out why she was helping me. When we stood up again and were about to leave, I said, "I'll never be able to thank you enough ... without you I would have been done for... Now there's maybe a bit of hope, only a little, but still... Even Lucky Luke's leaving me in peace."

Now she was looking serious. She wound her hair around her finger and visibly blushed.

"Well," she replied, "believe me, there will be a way you can repay me, even more than you can imagine!"

This was extremely mysterious, but I didn't try to delve deeper, because that's not in my nature. With me, what you see is what you get.

"I've got to get a move on," she said, "or I'll be late for my music lesson."

"You're still learning?"

She stopped suddenly. Behind her, high up in the sky, I saw some migrating birds fly past in a triangle. Maybe it was an isosceles triangle, maybe not. Christmas wasn't far off.

"I've got to go on learning because at the end of the year I want to take a very important audition. It's crucial that I pass."

"And what will you do after this audition?"

"I'll go to a special college where I can study music as well as doing schoolwork."

We went our separate ways. My heart was in turmoil: it felt as though it was swelling up and might burst at any moment. As I walked along the edge of the park, I found a blackbird on the ground, spread flat out and shivering all over. Its poor beak, like a yellow comma, was half open jast as if it was pleading for help. It looked exactly how I felt inside, and I'm sure that's what aroused my compassion and love of animals. When I picked up the little bird, it seemed as heavy as a ball of lead. I thought this was probably to do with density, because living things have to shrink into themselves when they're suffering deeply, so that there is less room for unhappiness to take hold.

I ran home carrying the little parcel of life huddled inside its feathers. I wasn't optimistic about the chances of saving the creature. I wasn't much of an expert on blackbirds, but it looked like this one was in a lot of trouble.

Etienne and Marcel had been there for ages, but I still took the time to settle my patient into an old shoebox, lined with cotton wool, and offer him some breadcrumbs soaked in milk. But he wouldn't eat anything. Etienne and Marcel had got their instruments ready in the workshop and while they were waiting for me they'd been talking to Dad, who was tinkering with the Panhard's engine. He was giving them a detailed tour, holding a valve torsion bar, and he reminded me of a king with his sceptre. King of the Panhard, if you like.

"You're here! What kept you? We were just about to leave!"

I used the blackbird as an excuse for being late, so then they teased me a bit on the subject of animals, reminding me of the frog debacle. I tried to get them involved in my life-saving enterprise by asking them why the creature wouldn't eat.

"He's probably on hunger strike," said Etienne.

That made no sense at all to me.

I went to get my old electric guitar and tuned it as well as I could – *mi la re sol ti mi*, or something like that. Anyway, it wasn't important.

Etienne had composed a new piece and I'd put some words to it. We began to play, but my heart wasn't in it. I felt really feeble, as if I was holding a crankshaft rather than a musical instrument. The other two were writhing about all over the place and didn't notice anything, because obviously they hadn't had the benefit of the musical and aesthetic education that I now had. We finished the demo because we wanted to send it to a record company. What I was dreading was the possibility that they might talk about it at school. How would that make me look in front of Marie? I'd have cut my hand off rather than pick up an instrument in front of her. I'd told them it would be better to keep quiet about our musical mayhem, because people might get jealous. Etienne and Marcel didn't really buy this because they wanted to do a concert at the school Christmas fair, just before the holidays.

"The thing is," said Etienne, "there's nothing better than music for pulling girls!"

106

When we left the workshop, it was completely dark and it had got cold too. The sky was sprinkled with stars. I thought that Marie was probably still grinding away at her cello and I almost felt like going to meet her after her music lesson. I told Etienne and Marcel that I had to revise some geometry, because the next day there was a test on cones, pyramids, spheres and that sort of thing.

"We don't give a stuff about cones and pyramids," said Marcel, "and one of these days we're going to nick old Hopalong's crutches and make flutes out of them. Then she won't be able to bug us any more."

Etienne burst out laughing.

"You don't know what you're talking about," I said, "it's not funny to have to carry your dead baby around in your right leg."

They stared at me with eyes like great big marbles. They just didn't get it: I could see they thought I was mad. I felt even more respect for my dear Egyptian, who'd understood exactly what I meant. Then they explained that anyway they couldn't care less about school because they'd found their vocation. A poultry farmer they knew had told them that no one had ever been able to invent a machine for cutting chicken breasts off the carcass. So chicken breast cutters were in demand. But because time is money, the factories sent the chickens down a sort of conveyor belt and right-handers cut out the chicken breasts on the left-hand side while left-handers cut out the chicken breasts on the right-hand side. The factories were short of left-handers and so paid them a lot more. And Etienne and Marcel were both left-handed. Since they'd discovered this option, they'd stopped studying altogether and their reports for the first term had been even more catastrophic than usual.

"We're all right, our future career's sorted out!"

I thought they lacked ambition. Personally, I was trying to get myself back on track. And maybe one day I'd even end up having some ambition myself. Just a little. They went off on their bikes into the night. Dad was putting ticks against advertisements in the *Journal for Collectors and the Curious*. I sat down on the edge of the sofa and looked at him. For the first time I thought that there was something wistful about his eyes, a sort of sadness in his face. It felt like it was up to me to protect him, but from what exactly I wasn't sure. It was one of the first times in my life when I felt a little bit of strength and confidence, and when I realized that other people weren't as strong as I'd thought. It wasn't as good a feeling as I'd imagined it would be. In the end, being aware of other people's weakness doesn't make you feel any stronger.

I turned on the radio to listen to the news, which was about a plane crash in Russia. The pilot and the co-pilot had been arguing about one of the flight attendants, who couldn't make up her mind between the two of them. As a result the plane went down nose first.

"They're idiots, the Russians," said Dad, conclusively, closing his magazine.

I went to have a look at my bird. I weighed him in my hands and he felt as heavy as ever. That didn't seem a good sign. Still, when I stroked his feathers I could feel him breathing. I scattered a few crumbs of bread by his beak and for a moment I had the feeling he was trying to smile at me.

Dad turned up to check out my animal rescue skills.

"Did you have a pet when you were little, Dad?"

"When I was twelve, my father brought back a puppy that one of his clients wanted to get shot of... Then, by the time I met your mother, he was a very old dog. Animals weren't really your mother's thing, you know ... especially old ones... I had to choose between him and her..."

109

"And then she was the one who got shot of you."

So he must understand about the love of animals, and animal rescue.

That evening, I remembered to revise my maths, but it was harder than usual, because I hadn't gone over the problem with Marie in the afternoon.

* * * *ABC is a triangle and F is the translation that maps A to B. I is the midpoint of AC. D and J are the respective images of C and I after translation F. Prove that J is the midpoint of BD.*

The three stars in the book were to show the level of difficulty. I struggled for quite a while, and tried not to lose heart, because that certainly wouldn't have impressed Marie. She never gave up with her cello, although it's a very difficult and obstinate instrument. And also I didn't want to end up cutting out chicken breasts, especially the ones on the left. I drew a slightly strange diagram with arrows going everywhere and I proved as best I could what they were asking me to prove.

There was also a poem to learn by heart. It was a very sad poem that an old poet had written when he was about to die. It began, "I am nothing but bones, a skeleton's double," and it finished, "Farewell, dear companions, farewell, my dear friends, I shall go first to prepare you the way." Before, I really hadn't liked poetry and I'd never managed to learn the poems the teachers gave us. It always seemed to me that people who made things extra difficult for themselves when they wrote must be really screwed up. But I thought this poem was beautiful. It reminded me of my poor blackbird, who was in a similar predicament, and also of the music that Marie played, which was composed in the same period as the poem. It must have been a very sad time, when people went blind for no good reason. Nothing like the time of the musketeers. I went to find Dad, so that I could recite the poem to him. I took great pains to say the last line in a very poignant way, closing my eyes as if it was I who was dying.

"What cheery stuff they're teaching you!" he said. "That poet Ronsard's got a nerve, writing all those centuries ago and still making us feel depressed even now!"

"Not everything has to be cheerful," I said. "For example, music isn't always happy either. I'm not talking about the racket The Rattletraps make, obviously... But the cello, for instance, real music, that can be sad too, but it still gives you a good feeling."

He gave me a slightly amused look.

"My word, Victor, your intellect is really coming along."

I was startled, because those words exactly reflected what I felt too, deep down. Although you can't admit things like that to yourself.

Then he said, thoughtfully, "It's true as well... I wonder why we like listening to sad music..."

"Perhaps it stops us feeling so alone with regard to existence and all that sort of thing. Perhaps the most difficult thing in life is to feel alone."

"I'm pleased to see you having such profound thoughts..."

He was looking amused again.

"It's because of my profound thoughts that becoming a chicken breast cutter doesn't appeal to me. Right or left. If you get me."

In the street in front of the house a workman, perched on the platform of a small crane, was putting up garlands of Christmas lights.

6

The next morning, there was a dusting of white snow everywhere. The school bus skidded and everyone screamed, as though we were on a roller coaster. The driver turned scarlet, but we couldn't tell if it was from fear or anger. I saw on the school noticeboard that lots of the teachers were having trouble getting in. Haisam told me that the first lesson was cancelled and invited me to his father's lodge. My friend had got even fatter and I imagined that one day he'd completely fill the lodge, be trapped inside and condemned to play chess for all eternity. They'd reached the fifth round of the 1962 Curaçao tournament.

"Bobby Fischer against Viktor Korchnoi," explained Haisam.

Out of the window I could see the other kids

113

building a snowman in the playground. I looked out for Marie, but there was no sign of her.

"It's the Pirc Defence," added Haisam's father, "played for the first time in Nuremberg in 1883."

"You see, my friend," whispered Haisam, "the aim of the strategy is clear: the white knight goes to b3 and is then chased away by a5-a4, possibly followed by a3, which obviously weakens the a1-h8 diagonal, where the bishop g7 is lurking. Obviously. It's elementary really..."

"Obviously!" I agreed, so as not to look like a dimwit. "Very elementary."

The snowman in the playground was getting bigger.

"Now: 13.g4! An aggressive move that seems to turn the tables, but wait for Korchnoi's spectacular response..."

It seemed to me that chess, like music, was mostly a question of language.

After the game, I asked the Honourable Egyptian to look over my maths.

"I drew a weird thingy and then I tried to prove it as best I could."

"Let's have a look."

He put his work down next to mine. And this is what they looked like:

His:

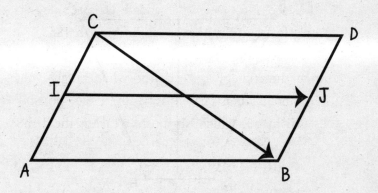

Proof

B and D are the respective images of A and C after translation F. The image of the line segment AC after translation F is therefore the line segment BD. I is on the line AC, therefore its image J is on the line BD.

I is the midpoint of AC, therefore IA = IC.

Translation preserves lengths, so JB = IA and JD = IC.

Therefore JB = JD.

If a point is on the line BD and is equidistant from B and D, it must be the midpoint of the line segment BD.

<u>Conclusion</u>: J is the midpoint of BD.

Mine:

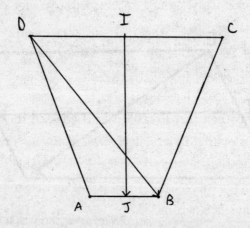

<u>Proof</u>:

ABC is a triangle with one invisible side. I is the middle of the line BC. The invisible side AC touches the line IJ and the line DB.

<u>Conclusion</u>: J is more or less in the middle of the line BD.

Frankly, they didn't have a lot in common. My work didn't look much like anything at all. I've noticed that it's often by comparison that mistakes become mistakes. I looked anxiously at Haisam. He showed my work to his father, who pulled a strange face as he put away the chess pieces.

"Did you do this on your own?" Haisam asked.

"Yes!" I said proudly.

"Oh, I see! That explains it."

It was then that I realized he'd guessed the whole business with Marie. There was really no point in trying to hide anything from my honourable friend.

"You'd better ask her to help you revise geometry."

"Why? Is it wrong?"

"Totally. But it's quite funny. It's even funnier than the real thing ... *one invisible side...* That's quite something!"

He slid the paper in front of me.

"Read me your conclusion. I think I must be hallucinating."

"Well, yes, OK: 'Conclusion: J is more or less in the middle of the line BD.' Personally, I think it has a certain style."

Haisam looked dismayed.

"You need to understand that 'more or less' doesn't exist in maths... Here, copy down the solution."

And that was when I said completely the wrong thing.

"Are you sure it's right?"

I thought the world was going to stop turning on its axis and the snowman in the playground was going to melt away all in one go. Haisam's father dropped all the chess pieces on the floor and they both stared at me as though I was some really peculiar creature. The Turkish father of my Egyptian friend made a triangle shape with his fingers and said, in an icy voice, "So you think, do you, that the people who built the pyramids would have trouble drawing a simple triangle?"

I wasn't too sure whether he was joking or whether he was actually expecting a reply, but he looked as though something was coming to the boil inside him. It didn't look good: I thought he was about to blow up.

"Don't be angry, I was joking, obviously I was joking."

"Well, it was a joke in very poor taste. Here, have some Turkish delight."

He mulled it over for a few seconds and then broke his silence.

"Good grief!"

And on that note Haisam and I went back to join our classmates. As we waited in line, I gave a little wave to Marie and then, as usual, when we went inside I took my seat next to hers. While the teacher was doing the register, she whispered to me, "Did you do the maths exercise?"

"Yes."

"It wasn't too hard?"

"Yes, but I did what I could."

"Let's see."

I hesitated, but the temptation was too strong, and I slipped her the copy I'd made of Haisam's work.

"Well done! You've made amazing progress. Soon you won't need me any more."

"Don't say that, just as I'm really starting to need you."

I went as red as a tomato, first because I'd given her the copy of Haisam's work and second because of what I'd said. And now it was I who wanted to withdraw from the world like a wounded animal. I swivelled round and saw my honourable friend at the back of the class, smiling affectionately despite all the "invisible sides" and "more or lesses" that filled my life. And I thought he looked like the snowman in the playground.

At the end of break, the school loudspeaker blared out that Marie and I were required in Lucky Luke's office. When we were both outside the door, I knocked. Lucky Luke opened it and told us to sit down. He didn't seem at all angry. It was quite a while since he and I had had any setbacks. Alexandre Dumas had brought us closer, and we were enjoying a sort of honeymoon.

"We've got a problem!" he said straight away.

"A problem with us?" asked Marie.

Personally, I was trying to say as little as possible, because you never know.

"Yes, a problem with you, but it's not your fault. Or at least not your fault, young lady. Victor?"

"Yes, sir."

"First I want you to swear something to me…"

"Yes, what?"

"That you had nothing to do with the two snowmen in the playground."

"In that case, I can swear on whatever you like … on the memory of Alexandre Dumas, say, or even on the music of Johann Sebastian Bach… You can't ask for more than that! And anyway I couldn't have had anything to do with the snowmen because I was with Haisam and his father replaying Curaçao 1962."

"Curaçao 1962? That sounds like an alcoholic drink."

"No, no, it's a chess tournament," Marie cut in. "It was won by Petrosian, the master of impenetrable defence."

"That's exactly right," I added, just for the sake of it. "But anyway, what snowmen are you talking about?"

Lucky Luke was floundering. He seemed to be asking himself whether it was really me sitting in front of him.

"Well, all right, here's the thing; there are two snowmen in the playground – actually, I should say a snowman and a snow-woman."

He pulled the curtain aside with a flourish. He was right. The original snowman was no longer alone and now sported a carrot in a place that left no doubt as to his gender. At the tip of the carrot, almost touching it, were the snow-woman's buttocks.

"Hey, it's not bad!" I said.

Lucky Luke let the curtain fall back.

"I'm sorry," said Marie, "but I don't see what it's got to do with us."

"It's got something to do with you because we found these placards around the necks of the two ... characters."

And he took out two placards. Someone had

121

written on them with a marker: VICTOR + MARIE.

All I could say was, "The scumbags!"

Marie burst out laughing.

"Victor, do you know who could have done this?" asked Lucky Luke.

I had a pretty good idea, but I chose to keep it to myself.

Marie couldn't stop laughing. As soon as she calmed down a bit she started up again. She couldn't help herself.

I was furious.

"Fine," I said. "Now the whole school thinks we're an item…"

"It's just childish nonsense, Victor," said Lucky Luke, kindly. "Don't worry about it. But I promise that if we find the guilty party, he'll be severely punished."

"I should hope so. I've got my self-respect to think about. If we can't count on the authorities in this school any more…"

Lucky Luke seemed amused. He showed us to the door as though we were important guests. Marie was in a hurry to get away, because she needed to prepare the visual aids for her presentation on the book about Helen Keller's life, so I found myself alone with Lucky Luke.

"Really," I said, "I don't understand her. Anyone would think this business means nothing to her."

"She lives in a different world... You know, she could have gone into the sixth form early, but she's too young and they wouldn't take her..."

"Why isn't she in a special school for people who are geniuses like her?" I asked.

"I don't know. We suggested it and her parents agreed, but she didn't. She's chosen instead to audition for a music school. It has a very good reputation – it's highly selective."

"How classy!"

For a moment I thought he was going to burst out laughing. *Great*, I thought, *he's taking the mick out of me.*

"By the way, I hadn't realized you were a musician too."

My jaw dropped in surprise.

"How come you know that?"

"Etienne and Marcel came by this morning to ask if you could do a concert at the Christmas fair."

"And?"

"And I said yes. For once they've come onto my radar for something good. So we can look forward to our first performance by Victor the guitar hero... What genre of music do you play?"

123

"The screwed-up spring-loaded metal genre, if you really want to know. How soon is the fair?"

"In a fortnight, just before the holidays."

The bell started ringing.

"Got to go," I said.

"First, I've got something to ask you… Are you sure that Alexandre Dumas wrote *The Three Musketeers* all on his own?"

"Why shouldn't he have?"

"Because I've heard some strange rumours about it. Plus it's seriously long… And since he wrote dozens like that, I was wondering…"

"I've no idea. I'll find out if you like?"

"Yes, because the uncertainty is spoiling my enjoyment of the book, you see."

I left and headed towards the stairs. But then I had an idea, so I turned back and knocked on Lucky Luke's office door again. He was already comfortably settled on the sofa, with his feet on his desk and his nose in *The Three Musketeers*.

"Tell me, sir, about the business with the snowmen, you do agree that we can't just let it go? Because otherwise it becomes a free-for-all and that's the road to ruin."

"It's strange to hear that coming from you, but

sure, I agree."

"If in revenge I remove the loo paper from the boys' toilets ... you won't give me a hard time?"

"I'll try to turn a blind eye, but at the first sign of faecal impaction I'll be obliged to launch an inquiry."

Impaction the state of being packed or wedged in. Faecal impaction: a solid, immobile bulk of human faeces that can develop in the rectum as a result of chronic constipation.

Serve them right, though, wouldn't it!

I arrived a little late for class, but given my progress and recent attentiveness, the teacher couldn't really make an issue of it. Marie was still preparing her visual aids for the presentation. She also had a board with loads of photos, quotes and text boxes.

I sat down and she began to talk to us about Helen Keller, who was a perfectly normal little American girl. When she was eighteen months old, she became desperately ill. That was down to fate. So then she could no longer see or hear anything at all. Obviously, put like that, it doesn't sound like such a big deal, and I was worried that Marie was taking a risk, because when it came to the boys in my class, that sort of thing was likely to make them crack up. But in fact, the way she spoke and her tone of voice gave them goosebumps, and the atmosphere was so tragic that no one felt like laughing or sneering at it. The phrase that came to me was that she had the class "wrapped around her little finger". Actually I was quite pleased with this expression.

At the same time, Marie looked as though she might fall apart in the middle of her sentences, and it was impossible to tell whether this was a sign of great strength or extreme weakness. In this way, she helped us to visualize Helen, who was trapped in silence and darkness until her parents took on a specialist teacher to help her. The most curious thing about it was that she accompanied her presentation with snatches of music on her cello. Marie said it was to represent Helen's state of mind and to help us imagine what it would be like to live in darkness and silence. The instrument sounded as though it was howling on its own in a dark place. I couldn't remember ever having heard her play those pieces. Sometimes it seemed to me that the notes were smashing to the ground, like birds falling from an electric wire. It gave us the shivers, that's all there was to it.

I looked at the teacher, who was in a corner of the room with her hand over her mouth and seemed to be trying to stop herself from weeping or crying out. It was almost frightening how solemn and silent the class was.

Thanks to her teacher, Helen began to make progress. She learnt to tap words in her parents' hands and when she tapped "daddy" into her father's hand, well, he burst into tears. Normally it's comments like this that turn the class into a tribe of barbarians. It's hard to believe but this time the boys were mesmerized, and the girls too: everyone seemed to be following Marie's lips, or the bow as it slid over the strings like a tightrope walker on a steel wire.

Sometimes Marie spoke so softly that we were all struggling to read her lips, and I realized of course that she was putting us in Helen's shoes again. In the end, her teacher did such a good job that Helen managed to pass a very difficult exam – so difficult that no girl had dared to even think of attempting it before. Then she travelled up and down the country to explain the importance of helping blind and deaf children, because of a sentiment known as compassion.

To finish with, Marie recited a bizarre sort of poem all about how vowels have colours. She punctuated each verse with very violent bow strokes, blasting out like atomic flashes. Everyone was blown away, but for me it was something special. I felt a bit like I'd been part of this poetic journey, as though we'd done it hand in hand. And at the end of the journey, I thought again about what I'd said to Marie only an hour earlier: that it was now that I was really starting to need her.

She finished the poem just before the bell rang. The teacher only had time to stammer that she was lost for words at the moment, that we all needed time to recover, but that she'd never before been punched in the stomach in such a beautiful way. I thought she was right: sometimes art is like being in a boxing ring, where the punches raise you up before they knock you out. We were all a bit dazed as we went out into the corridor.

"You all look like you've been hit by a tornado," said Etienne. "Did the teacher have a go at you?"

I took the opportunity to challenge him about the concert at the Christmas fair. I was less and less keen to show myself up in front of Marie, but I wasn't going to admit that.

"You'll have to go ahead without me!" I said as we walked down the crowded staircase.

"You can't do that to us."

"And why not?"

"Because you can't just chuck away months of work. And anyway we've made a commitment to Lucky Luke. A band's got to stick together."

We went out into the playground. The kids were running round and round the two snowmen, whooping loudly. Clearly the Metro couldn't be expected to understand that musically speaking I had now discovered a different world. These days I was receiving an aesthetic education that made me look at things in a new light. There was another kind of music. It seemed to come from another planet, far away and inaccessible, and it made my heart swell. I was perfectly happy to go on making a racket with the Metro, since I wasn't capable of anything better, but I'd have preferred us to keep it to ourselves.

Etienne went on talking about the concert and suggested that we should all dress in white. Then Marcel turned up, looking shaken. He stared at us wide-eyed with distress, as though some great danger was lying in wait for him.

"You know what?" he asked.

"No."

"SOMEONE has hidden the toilet paper again!"

Naturally I put on a shocked face.

"It's been a while since that happened!" I said. "I wonder who on earth it could be..."

"I bet it's a girl," said Marcel. "Only a girl would do something as mean as that!"

"Tough times ahead!"

"There's a risk of impaction!" I said, to impress everyone.

"What?"

"Impaction. Faecal impaction, in fact!"

"What's that?"

"Why don't you look it up in the dictionary, under the letter F. And the letter I."

I didn't say anything more because just at that moment, a snowball smashed into my nose. It hurt like hell, as if I'd been hit by a stone. Drops of blood began to splatter onto the snow. I immediately noticed the big bloke laughing near the snowmen: a guy from Year Ten who strutted about everywhere as though he was proud of his small, squashed-looking thug's face. I hadn't let him join The Rattletraps, and ever since then he'd held a grudge and was out to get me at any opportunity. He'd been sniffing around me in the corridors and the playground for a while, but I'd always managed to keep my head down and my fists stuffed deep in my pockets.

All at once it became crystal clear to me that he was responsible for the snowmen. I'd had good reason to suspect him right from the start. Now there was no doubt about it. I thought about going straight off to find Lucky Luke, but when he added insult to injury by yelling out some not very nice stuff about Marie and me, I saw red. It was like instantaneous global warming. I hurtled across the playground, spraying drops of blood like Hansel and Gretel scattering breadcrumbs. My fingers were tingling like they used to when I was younger and went to boxing classes.

Out of the corner of my eye I saw Haisam stretching out a great paw to hold me back, and I heard Etienne yelling, "Don't be an idiot!" But I'd shot off like a torpedo; nothing could stop me. I threw myself at the guy's neck and wrapped my thighs around his waist, squeezing as hard as I could. He began to bellow like a pig about to be slaughtered. I had time to get a close-up view of his red pimples and to think how gross they were. We fell to the ground, locked together. He tried to break free but my thighs gripped him firmly, as if I had him in a vice. I thought I might cut him in half. Then one of his

131

ears came into my line of sight and I bit it hard. After that I let go.

"He's ripped my ear off, the animal!"

"And he's bust my nose! And a tooth too, the jerk!"

I was laying it on a bit thick, but I wanted to show that I'd been injured too. And I hadn't even got started on the moral injuries.

In the end we were both led off, him by a teaching assistant to see the nurse, and me by my Egyptian friend to the caretaker's lodge. Haisam stuffed some cotton wool up my nose, which made me look like a sheep's head in a butcher's shop with parsley coming out of its nostrils. It also made me talk like a duck. I began to feel a bit better. I thought again about the question Lucky Luke had put to me.

"Haisam, I've got something important to ask you."

"Go ahead, but I'm going to have trouble taking you seriously looking like that."

"Do you know if Alexandre Dumas wrote his books on his own, or did he have collaborators?"

He seemed surprised and raised his eyebrows. He took a moment to put away the cotton wool in the first-aid cupboard before he replied.

"It would take more than one life just to *copy out*

all his books. He must have had many collaborators, and almost certainly ghostwriters too."

"Ghostwriters?"

"Yes, people who write books for other people to put their name to. It's very common in literature."

"What if the writer really was a ghost? What would you call the person who wrote his book for him?"

"Why do you always have to complicate everything?"

He was right. I always made things difficult.

He thought for a moment.

"And actually it's true it's not that straightforward, since Alexandre Dumas also wrote some ghost stories."

"There, so you see," I said, "things are complicated."

But I didn't come across as particularly authoritative, because of the tufts of cotton wool coming out of my nostrils.

Then Lucky Luke came to get me and I followed him to his office.

I sat down in the same place I'd been sitting when he'd called Marie and me in that very morning.

"You've had a piece of luck!"

"Do you think so?" I said, pointing at the cotton

wool in my nose, which was making me cross-eyed. It wasn't what I called lucky!

"Yes. If your friend Marie hadn't come to speak to the Head, I think you might well have been suspended."

"She did that?"

"Yes. And to explain your aggressive behaviour she gave us this: it was in the snowball."

He opened his fist and flicked a stone into his hand, like a tennis ball.

"Legitimate self-defence, then?"

"Possibly ... but you'll still get a warning about the ear."

"Sorry to change the subject, but I found the answer to your question about Alexandre Dumas."

His eyes lit up, as though we were finally coming on to a serious subject.

"And so?"

"And so, things are a bit complicated, according to my sources. But well, anyway, to sum up, I can confirm that he wrote all his books on his own. On his own from beginning to end. He was not the type to have ghostwriters, even though he wrote ghost stories! If you get me."

"I knew it. What a guy! Not one of these constipated

134

little writers you get these days who want a Nobel Prize for squeezing out a hundred pages."

By the time I got home I had a splitting headache. A whole army was goose-stepping inside my skull, with the artillery and air power coming up behind. But I still went to see my blackbird in his shoebox. The breadcrumbs were gradually disappearing. It was a good sign. He must have been pecking at them while no one was watching. It made me think that wounded blackbirds must need to withdraw from the world too. I held him in the palm of my hand. It felt like holding a little portable heart. He was both really light and very heavy at the same time, which is quite hard to explain.

Dad got me some aspirin and I stretched out on the sofa, underneath a blanket, while he prepared the following month's edition of the *Journal*. Then we turned on the TV. We selected a culture channel because now, with the education I was getting, and also thanks to Marie opening my eyes to culture, I couldn't let things slide.

It was an evening of programmes dedicated to the Second World War, and especially to the deportation of the Jews, who were put in camps of some sort, where they were worked into the ground and then killed. There were pictures of whole populations leaving their houses and walking in lines to the railway stations, overseen by guards. Then all of them – men, women and children – were forced to climb into the trains and taken to who knows where. I tried to get Dad to explain. I asked him if all those people knew what they were in for, and why they didn't run away.

"They must have thought they were just going to be made to work," replied Dad. "They didn't realize they were in such danger. Who could have imagined it?"

"But Dad, for a start it's not that great to work for nothing... And secondly, all those people, they must surely have realized that the locals were hostile..."

"After being beaten by rifle butts and whatnot, they surely must have realized in the end. But they could never have dreamt that they were going to be annihilated like that. Why would they have thought that, when they'd done nothing wrong? And then, you know, they were dying of hunger in the ghettos, everything was in turmoil..."

"Ghettos?"

Dad pointed at the dictionary on the table.

I understood what he was getting at. I hunted for the word... Ghetto, ghetto ... there it was:

Ghetto *Jewish quarter; district where Jews were forced to live.*

"They were no more naïve or submissive than anyone else, but when they were told that they'd be better off in specially built camps than in the ghettos, well, many of them believed it. And anyway, what choice did they have?"

I let my thoughts travel back into the distant past. My grandfather had also come from the East. And it occurred to me that by getting to France just before the war, he'd escaped all the dangers that we'd seen on the TV screen.

"Dad, do you think Grandpa came from that part of Europe?"

"Yes, not very far from there. He left the village of Lemberg, in Galicia, to escape the pogroms. Then he travelled through Poland, Hungary, Romania..."

My eyes followed Dad's finger through the air as it traced Grandpa's journey across Europe.

"Progammes? What kind of programmes?"

"Pogroms, you noodle. Organized persecution, if you like."

"And so he escaped, your father, because he travelled west?"

"Yes, he got away."

"So, hey, it was by following the sun that Grandpa managed to avoid all that!"

I was quite proud of having an ancestor who'd got out of difficulties by hitching his fortunes to the sun. I thought it was a smart way to stay alive.

Dad began to leaf through the Krebs manual, but I felt like staying a bit longer with him and reminiscing about the past.

"Say, Dad, did Grandpa talk to you about his travels and about arriving in France?"

Dad put the manual down on his knees.

"He said very little about his journey, because he was obsessed with the idea of seeming more French than the French. He used to fill his face with French food like beef bourguignon and cassoulet, so as to forget the stuffed carp and red cabbage he used to eat in the East."

"So he was a sort of survivor of great tragedies?"

"Yes, a survivor. That's exactly right."

"Like us, Dad, basically we're sort of survivors too."

He smiled, with his head on one side, and then he buried himself in his Krebs bible.

I fell into a doze, lulled by the random images that were still going through my head. I thought that thanks to Marie I was a survivor of the education system as well. I dreamt that I was on a big deserted ocean liner, walking on a vast, very well polished deck. Suddenly, I came face to face with a herd of cattle, just like that, who looked as though they were loose but in fact were surrounded by barbed wire. Then a siren went off and I found myself leaning over the rail looking at one of the cows that had been thrown into the still, calm sea, shining like molten lead. I searched for a lifebelt to throw to the cow, which was sinking fast, although it looked like it was being swallowed by sand or mud rather than water. Then I realized that the disappearing cow didn't have any eyes, just two red holes.

I was drifting away in Dad's arms as he carried me up to my bedroom and I didn't want to wake up properly. But I still had time to think that it would soon be my birthday and that life might not be so bad, after all.

7

My stunt in the playground had given me a certain status at school. It's not every day you see a person defending his honour by taking a chunk out of someone's ear. Luckily, it wasn't too serious – just a matter of sewing the bully's dangling earlobe back on. Since his ear had to be protected for the next two weeks with a big bandage, I took to calling him Van Gogh. Even the teachers seemed to be taking me more seriously and seeing me in a different way: perhaps from slightly less high up and more on the same plane.

Now, of course, as far as the whole school was concerned, Marie and I were married, with a big house, two cars and three children. People knew I was a bit touchy about it, and because they didn't want to lose their ears, they didn't dare tease us too much about our relationship. One day, when I was in the lodge with Haisam, he said something that pleased me, and should have intrigued me too.

"You have to admit, it's pretty impressive, what she's done…" Then he added, "Marie's discovered the secret to making you more *alive*."

But he was a hopeless case: he just couldn't take his eyes off the chessboard.

"Hmm, that's odd…" he murmured, absent-mindedly.

"What's odd this time?"

"Well, you remember the 1922 Rubinstein-Tarrasch endgame – from the Dutch Defence?"

"Of course I remember," I said, just to play along.

"I'd never noticed that by playing h8 on his twenty-sixth move, Rubinstein won a piece with Qe7. Stupid of me, huh?"

"How will you ever forgive yourself?"

His eyes smiled at me behind his big spectacles. He looked enormous in the little lodge: he made me think of a mythical creature. Perhaps he'd take over from his father and stay there all his life. After all, Dad had taken El Dorado over from his father. And maybe I'd follow the same pattern. I suddenly thought of Haisam's symbolic drawing, the one I'd found in my rucksack on the first day of school: an apple tree with big red apples lying all around the trunk. When he'd given it to me, he'd said, "The apple never falls very far from the tree."

"What does that mean?" I'd asked.

"It's a parable. One day you'll understand."

"One of those big umbrellas? Are you kidding me?"

"No, you dope, that's a parasol. Look it up in the dictionary."

That evening, I'd followed his advice.

Parable *a simple story or statement designed to illustrate a puzzling moral or spiritual lesson.*

I could see it was puzzling, that's for sure, but apart from that I had absolutely no idea what my dear Egyptian was going on about with his apple tree and his apples.

Haisam was always finding really deep ideas in totally unexpected places. And then he'd come up with exactly the right words to express their deepness. When he'd said, "Marie's discovered the secret to making you more *alive*," that was just what I felt myself. I hadn't become "more intellectual" as

Dad had put it – and as I'd thought too – but "more alive". And that's something much more important. Sometimes, it seemed to me that my eyes had never been fully open before. I felt I could now focus on things and on the world in general, as though all through my life I'd been looking through a fuzzy lens.

And so, after a while, I began to feel really confident in some subjects. I even participated in class and contributed knowledgeable comments to the lessons. Usually, these were suggestions that Marie had made while we were working together, but I think it was only my friend Haisam who guessed.

But it was the approaching Christmas fair and The Rattletraps' concert that was really stressing me out. Luckily, Etienne and Marcel wanted to keep the musicians' identity a secret. Being masters in the art of cheesy ideas, they'd cobbled together a poster showing the silhouettes of three musicians with question marks instead of heads. They were stuck up all over the school. One day, when Marie and I were walking past a row of these posters, she asked me, "Do you know what kind of music they're going to play?"

"Rock, I should think, or something of the sort..."

"You'll probably laugh at me, but listening to stuff like that is absolute torture for my ears. I can't bear it, just like I can't bear liver. What about you, do you like that kind of thing?"

"Liver or rock bands?"

"Both."

I nearly spilled the beans and told her that she was looking at the founder of The Rattletraps, and what's more I played guitar and sang for them, but in the end I chickened out.

"I've never tasted liver," I replied. "As for rock musicians, they're just a bunch of jokers. As far as I'm concerned, playing music without being able to read the notes, well, I just don't get it. It's like swimming without water, for goodness' sake! Or French skipping without the skip!"

I should have taken the opportunity to own up to everything. She probably would have teased me a bit, or maybe not, but in any case it wouldn't have been much worse than that.

This business about the concert that Etienne and Marcel had organized was seriously beginning to worry me. They wanted us to come onstage dressed as Zorro and throw our masks into the audience during

the first chords of a song called "Hittin' the Wall" –
words and music by me. They thought this was a
phenomenal idea, but I couldn't help feeling slightly
ashamed at the prospect of connecting everything up
to 220 volts and flailing around as though we had
batteries up our bums, when for centuries there'd
been geniuses – including deaf and blind ones –
who'd dedicated their whole lives to coming up with
sounds that actually hung together.

I was thinking about all this during sport on
Friday afternoon. I had plenty of time, because we
were supposed to be long-distance running, and
distances offer an excellent opportunity to mull
things over. I'd decided to stop hiding behind the
plane trees like I used to do in the old days, even
though I found it hard. From time to time I looked
back to see if my dear Haisam was keeping up.
There he was, struggling along, sweating heavily
and wheezing. He looked enormous in the middle
of the track and his little eyes were screwed up
behind his steamed-up spectacles. I felt bad for him,
but he was still smiling broadly. He raised his big
paw when I turned round, as though to signal that
despite this ordeal, everything was OK, and we'd
soon be back together.

I was about to zoom around the last bend when I saw Marie walking in the opposite direction, on the grass at the edge of the track. I waved at her, but got no reaction at all. Yet I was sure she was looking straight at me. I wondered whether I'd offended her, or whether she'd found out about my involvement in the concert, or even if Van Gogh had been bad-mouthing me – I wouldn't have put it past him. If that was the case, I'd take a chunk out of his other ear, and that would be the end of it. When the sports lesson was over, I got changed as quickly as possible and dashed off. I finally caught up with Marie when she was almost home.

"Are you angry?" I asked her.

"Of course not, why should I be?"

"Because earlier you walked right past me and I waved to you and … it was as though you didn't recognize me!"

There was a strange look in her eyes: they seemed both transparent and cloudy at the same time and made me think of the eyes of the stuffed animals I'd seen in the Natural History Museum. She pulled a small gift-wrapped parcel out of her pocket.

"Here, this is for your birthday! See, I'm not angry at all."

Strangely enough, that had completely slipped my mind. I felt choked. I tried to think of a historical quote or something a bit intellectual to say, but I couldn't think of anything at all.

"Open it."

It was a model replica of a 1954 Panhard Dyna. It had everything: the three-spoked steering wheel, the elaborate enamelled Dyna logo on the bonnet, the curving rear axle joined to the Silentbloc shock absorbers, the long parallel stitched seams on the bench seat. I looked at Marie and thought I might start blubbing, right there and then.

"Do you like it?"

She was going to have to stop, or I wouldn't be able to hold it together. All I wanted to do was head straight to my bedroom and get over my agitation in my own good time, with the Dyna pressed to my heart and only Dad to see me, because with him it was different.

"I can't think of anything I've ever liked so much!" I managed to stammer. "Do you know the engineers made a mistake on this Dyna? The chrome ashtray ... see, there, on the right-hand side of the dashboard ... well, it reflected on the windscreen in an annoying way. So no one bought it."

"Just because of that? Oh, by the way, I forgot to tell you my parents have invited you to lunch tomorrow."

"That wasn't the only thing wrong with it…" said Dad that evening. "For a start it was advertised as having six seats, whereas in fact it could fit four comfortably, possibly five, but no more than that…"

He was holding the little Dyna in the palm of his hand, gently turning it around.

"And also," he went on, "the gearbox wasn't brilliant, you had to be very precise about the gear changes and avoid revving the engine too much. The steering was a bit off on tight bends, and when you braked the whole thing shuddered. But it's a nice model you've got there. It's very accurate… Look, they've even reproduced the lighting under the bonnet. I wonder where on earth your friend got hold of it. It's a collector's item!"

I really thought I was going to explode with pride. I had steam coming out of every pore and sirens sounded with each beat of my heart.

"Anyway, I've got a present for you too. Maybe not quite such a beauty as the Dyna, but still, a present."

He held out a paper bag.

"Sorry, gift-wrapping isn't my strong point... Go on, open it!"

It was an old-style chrome shaving set, with a razor, a shaving brush and a bottle of aftershave. I was a bit surprised.

"Thanks, Dad – it's a really nice present."

"Do you like it?"

"Yes, Dad."

"Go and try it out now, if you like. Lots of men shave in the evening... Especially when they're planning a nocturnal excursion..."

I realized the moment had finally arrived: he was going to take me with him in the Panhard to help with his deliveries.

So, I tried to shave off what there was, which was nothing at all really. But nothing will turn into something, I said to myself. I rubbed in some aftershave, just for the sake of it, and came out of the bathroom with my face all shiny. A man who's had a shave, that's quite something. My father looked at me very seriously.

"You know that Jews believe you become a man at thirteen?"

"But we're not Jewish, Dad."

He seemed to give this some thought, as though he had questions in his mind.

"Anyway, thirteen is a good age to become a man, Jewish or not," he said.

"Definitely."

"Shall we go?"

"Yes, Dad."

He picked up his address book and we set off in the Panhard. It felt like embarking on a long voyage on an ocean liner. We drove north through the night. Past deserted districts with clusters of tower blocks scattered here and there ... sprawling wastelands and empty warehouses ... suburban towns passing by one after the other. Gradually, Paris began to take shape around us. Buildings, allotments, a big hospital rearing up out of the darkness. All of a sudden we were in the city, which I thought of as a red heart, beating wearily. From that moment on, I lost track of where we were, and even who we were, to be honest, to say nothing of the time and the date... My father was jabbing at the gear lever. He looked like he knew where we were going, yet I couldn't help feeling that we'd lost our way and were going round in circles.

Now and again I thought about the meal at Marie's house and I sensed I was going to be tested. Red traffic lights in the darkness ... empty roads ... it was as though we were driving through an abandoned city. Occasionally we saw groups of people leaving cafés and restaurants and heard their shrill laughter fading into the night. Then, Dad brought the big car to a halt. We got out and walked along side by side for a few minutes, our footsteps ringing on the pavement. All at once he stopped, nudged me with his elbow and pointed out the street name: Rue de l'Echiquier. It was here that Dad's father had set up the legendary establishment known as El Dorado.

"Why is it called that, Dad?"

He explained to me that El Dorado was a mythical city of gold and great riches, thought to be hidden somewhere deep in South America. Dad stopped in front of an imposing metal shutter, then bent down to try and raise it. Nothing, it was jammed. Dad began to struggle with it, pulling with all his might, and that was when it occurred to me that one day he would leave me and I'd find myself standing all alone in front of a metal wall. But you have to keep going, even when you're carrying all these memories inside. The present is mostly about laying down memories, and there's something melancholy about that.

"Can I help you, Dad?"

He was still bending over, puffed out. He turned round and gave me a funny look. I couldn't tell if he was touched and looking at me with great fondness, or whether on the contrary he was cross that I'd suggested it.

"If you want… Hold on here and pull at the same time as me… One… Two—"

On the count of three the shutter shot right up, as if it weighed no more than a feather. Dad smiled at me but it gave me a strange feeling. To tell the truth, I'd have preferred it if he'd managed to raise it on his own. Sometimes it's hard to make sense of things.

"Well done! You see: you're a man now!"

He was giving me the thumbs-up, which is what he always did when he wanted to be super encouraging.

I smiled, in a lopsided sort of way.

The room inside was long and quite narrow. There were shelves running along the walls with crates of all sizes piled up on them. We were in El Dorado! At the back there was a spiral staircase leading up from the warehouse floor to the "admin office", as my father called it.

The office consisted of a wooden table and two dilapidated armchairs in a kind of corridor, with a few books on a little shelf and a huge map of Paris pinned to the wall. Dad sat down in one of the armchairs and suggested I sit opposite him. He crossed his legs and explained, with a serious look on his face, that he loved this place and it made him feel safe. It was here that his father had ended up hiding from the Germans during the war. He'd made a bad mistake thinking his worries would be over in France. At that time, the warehouse was a shop owned by a butcher who was also a collector and had acquired lots of rare pieces from him. He took my grandfather in when the Nasties were at his heels.

The strangest thing is that this butcher was Jewish, but he'd been very clever and specialized in making sausage and black pudding so no one had ever questioned him. And after the war, out of eternal gratitude, my grandfather had bought the shop from him and turned it into El Dorado, so that his friend could take early retirement from the butchery business.

Dad liked to come to his office and think things over, reflecting on life's problems and on decisions that needed to be made. He was in his element here. A coloured light blinked outside in the street and shone intermittently into the room. In the flickering shadows, the map was reflected onto my father's face, so that the streets and avenues actually seemed to become his veins.

I looked out of the window. The Panhard was waiting for us down below. A dusty rain was falling and the pavements had a glossy shine. I thought about Marie, and about that moment in the afternoon when she hadn't seemed to recognize me. I touched the Dyna 54 model car in my pocket. It felt as though the two of us, Marie and I, were joined together by a thin thread that evening.

"Dad?"

"Yes."

He was looking through copies of his magazine and planning the evening's itinerary. I could barely see him in the darkness.

"What does it feel like to be in love with someone?"

He looked up and cleared his throat. He was probably feeling like a wounded animal again.

"It feels like ... wait while I try and remember... It's like the end of exile."

"Exile – is that when you're far away from your country?"

"From your country, and from yourself as well. Does that make any sense to you?"

"Of course it does. Do you take me for a fool? But the thing that's bothering me is, when you're in love, does it feel the same whatever age you are?"

"Exactly the same. It's always the same old atomic bomb in a strawberry field. And you're the strawberry!"

"My friend Haisam thinks that if you never read any love stories you'll never fall in love."

"Tell him he knows nothing about it."

"I wouldn't dare, Dad ... but it doesn't matter, I've got plenty of time to form my own opinions. What are these books?"

I'd picked one out at random. Dad came up to me and looked over my shoulder.

"Oh, it's just an old story about a family... Nobody would read that nowadays ... about a father and son... No one's interested in that kind of thing any more... It's very badly written anyway..."

"Not like Alexandre Dumas."

"No, not like Alexandre Dumas. Shall we go?"

"Yes, Dad."

He showed me our itinerary on the big map. He mentioned place names that he seemed to know well, though they meant nothing to me at all. We went back down to El Dorado. A small light bulb cast a weak, yellowish light over the long narrow space, giving it a slightly dirty, tacky glow. My father gave me a long list of all the things we had to deliver. I had to read it out loud so that he could select the items from the shelves. It was funny to be walking together in the footsteps of my grandfather.

"An early edition of *Around the World in Eighty Days* by Jules Verne for the Blanchard brothers?"

"Done!"

I ticked the relevant item on my list.

"Ten copies of the guide to Versailles for Madame Michel?"

"OK, good!"

"A wooden leg that supposedly belonged to the actress Sarah Bernhardt, for Major General Rostand?"

"Got it!"

"A handwritten letter from Napoleon's regimental surgeon, for Doctor Marat?"

"Sorted!"

We loaded the packages into the Panhard.

"Do you think we make a good team, Dad?" I asked.

"Yes, we do make a good team," he replied, and I could hear the smile in his voice.

* * *

We set off again into the night. The Panhard was stuffed with parcels, like Father Christmas' sleigh. We wound our way around the town, backwards and forwards, in long complicated trails like strands of spaghetti. Again, I had the impression we were completely lost and would drive round and round for hours, as if the car was a wind-up toy. Dad talked to me about his magazine and his clients, extremely sensitive types who needed to be handled as carefully as dynamite, but his voice came to me from very far away. Sometimes I almost nodded off. Dad would leave me in the car and I'd watch him disappear through the entrance to a building carrying a big parcel. Once, in the middle of the night, I saw him come running out of a block of flats. From a balcony, a man in a dressing-gown was hurling insults at Dad, who threw himself at the Panhard like Noah rushing to get into the ark.

"What's his problem?" I asked.

Dad wiped his face with his big handkerchief.

"I don't know. It's always the same. When I leave him at the top everything's fine, he seems happy, and then everything must go haywire as I'm coming down the stairs. He can't help himself, he just *has* to insult me when I come out into the street."

157

We drove alongside the Botanic Gardens, all peaceful in the night, and then past the Lutetia Hotel.

"Do you remember the programme we watched the other evening about the concentration camps?" Dad asked.

"Yes, I remember – where they put the Jews…"

"Other people as well, but mostly Jews … well, when they came back from the camps – those that survived, that is – they ended up in this hotel…"

"It's a nice hotel … they must have been pleased! Were there enough rooms for everyone?"

"They weren't there on holiday, you little numbskull, they were gathered together there so that they could be reunited with their families, or so that they could be found somewhere to live."

"Like a kind of sorting station?"

"Perhaps."

"I talked to Haisam about that programme, because, you know, he's a sort of Egyptian Turkish Jew…"

"All those things at once?"

"Yes, all of them. It's because he's so intelligent, he doesn't need to respect normal boundaries. Although to be honest, I've never really understood how it works… He's not the talkative type… Anyway, when

I told him about the programme, he said he knew all about it and the Nasties…"

"The Nasties?"

"Yes, you know, the German soldiers, if you prefer…"

"The Nazis."

"Yes, OK, the Nazis … anyway, Haisam told me they made lampshades with the Jews' skin, and also stuffed pillows with their hair. I know Haisam is really intelligent and knows about almost everything, but this I didn't believe."

"You were wrong, because it's true."

"Oh, really?"

"Are you sure?" said Marie for the umpteenth time.

I was trying to be clever, reeling off the Dyna 54's technical data, which I'd got from my father. But she obviously wasn't interested in me blathering on. I thought again about the time she'd walked past me without giving any sign that she recognized me, as if I didn't exist. She was probably fed up with me trailing around after her. Even I thought I was a bit pathetic, especially when I caught myself trying out complicated musical terms to impress her.

I was holding the bunch of flowers I'd got for

her mother firmly in front of me. I'd hidden it in my bag, folded in four. It had been a good idea to choose artificial flowers. They're more expensive, but they last longer and at the end of the day they're equally elegant. And they give just as much pleasure, in my opinion. We were walking down the path towards the village. Stalls were being set up in a little square.

"Look," I said, "there's going to be a funfair."

Marie shrugged her shoulders. She seemed to be hiding under her mop of hair, which shone in the sunshine.

"What's the matter? It looks like you've got tears in your eyes."

"No, it's just pollen."

"Pollen? At Christmas?"

She smiled. But it was a wobbly smile.

"If you want," she said, "we could play Helen Keller."

Playing Helen Keller meant pretending to be blind and walking with your eyes shut while the other person told you where to go.

She began to walk forwards, her arms stretched out, like a sleepwalker. I ran behind her.

"Watch out for the postbox. Hard left … that's

it … now straight ahead … take a big step over the dog poo— Too late… Never mind, keep going…"

We stopped when we got to a bench near some men playing boules. The sky had turned grey and dull, as though it was about to snow.

"I've had enough of that stupid game," she said. "And anyway there's something I've got to tell you."

"I knew it."

"You knew what?"

"Well, I've been thinking that you've probably had enough of me trailing along after you. You play the cello, you've read everything…"

"And…?"

"Me, you see… Before I knew you, I couldn't even tell the difference between a cello and a violin. I even thought there was an instrument called a violent cello!"

"I don't see why that's relevant."

"It isn't. And, you see, I've only read the beginning of *The Three Musketeers*, and even then I skipped the descriptions. I need a ghost reader, not a ghostwriter! There's no need to giggle like that… Look, even the lousy flowers I'm giving to your mother, I don't know what kind they are. I only know they're made of fabric."

"You just find theoretical things difficult, that's all. It's always the same with ultra sensitive types like you."

"Really?"

"Yes, you lack the emotional detachment that would help you to see things objectively."

In front of us, one of the boules players had knocked away his opponent's ball and murmurs of admiration rolled towards us in a sort of wave. I almost decided to come clean about everything and tell her about The Rattletraps' concert, but I still had a shred of dignity left.

"You know all about Panhard cars," she said, "I'm sure no one else at school knows anything about them."

"That's of no use to anyone. They no longer exist, those cars. You never see them any more. And anyway, it's Dad who's the real expert. It was my uncle Zak who introduced him to them ages ago. Haisam, he's an expert in chess and emotional detachment. As for you, you know everything about everything. And I know nothing about anything. It's frustrating."

"Well, you're going to have an opportunity to feel useful, believe me. Because after what I'm about to tell you... Are you listening to me?"

"Yes, I'm listening."

I could sense that this was a serious moment, a bit like when Dad told me to go and have a shave. I felt I ought to look the part so I checked that my flies weren't undone. She was looking straight into my eyes, as though she wanted to nail me to the sky.

"OK, so here's the thing. Do you remember when I was away from school for a few days last month? I told you I'd been to visit an old aunt who was ill."

I didn't remember, but it didn't matter, it was no big deal.

"Yes, of course I remember. So it wasn't true?"

"No. The truth is that I was in hospital, in Paris. In a department that specializes in eyes."

I thought for a moment about the time when she passed me on the running track.

"Why? Have you got problems with your eyes?"

"Yes," she said simply.

"Like Johann Sebastian?"

I couldn't tell whether I'd been quite clever or utterly stupid to come up with this gem. In the square, the boules players were picking up their metal balls with a magnet on the end of a piece of string, so they didn't have to bend down. *How lazy is that!* I thought.

"I've got a disease which means that my sight is gradually getting worse. It's been going on for several years and now it's getting near the end. Already there are times when I can't see anything at all."

I was finding it more and more difficult to swallow my saliva, as if my mouth was filled with all the dust in the square.

"Yesterday, at the running track…"

"Yes, that's what it was. But I can sense that before long I'll be in darkness all the time."

I couldn't think of anything to say, and the more I tried to think of something, the harder it was.

"You're the only person I can tell," she said.

"Why? Your parents must be aware of it."

"They know about the disease of course. But it's still quite rare and no one has any idea – except me – when night will fall. Everyone thinks I've still got years to go."

"Surely something can be done… In Johann Sebastian's time, people went blind for no good reason … but it's different now… There must be some solution, there must be specialists. For all I know, there are even different specialists for the right and left eyes." *Like for chicken breasts*, I wanted to add.

"No. Believe me, I've studied the subject. I've even

164

been to conferences about it. Nothing can be done, nothing at all... The thing is ... I can't say anything to my parents ... because if I do I'll have to leave school before the end of the school year... I'll be sent to a specialist college and I won't be able to go to the music school..."

I didn't really understand, probably because, as she'd just told me, I lacked emotional detachment, which allows you to see and understand things clearly and objectively.

"Why would your parents stop you going to your music school? Don't they know that you're preparing for this audition?"

"Of course they do. They still hope I'll keep my sight, at least for many years yet. If they discover I'm blind they'll want to put me in this exclusive college that was created on purpose, after lots of research, to give disabled people like me the same chances as everyone else. Oh, of course they'll let me play on special occasions, but I heard them talking about it: if I lose my sight they'll put me where I'll be safe and they'll stop me from pinning all my hopes on a future in music."

"This situation is totally incendiary!" I murmured, scratching the back of my head.

"It's my only hope, you see. Getting to the month of June and passing the audition, whatever it takes. And once I've passed and the music school's given me a place, my parents won't be able to stop me... Don't you think?"

"Yes, definitely."

I don't know why, but I thought of Lucky Luke and his obsession with cycling.

"So basically we've broken away from the pack and we need to keep the lead until the end of the stage?" I said.

"That's it exactly."

"Well, it's going to be an exceptionally tricky mountain stage, we'll have to be prepared for that!"

Then I thought of my blackbird in his box full of cotton wool, with his little yellow beak half-open and his heavy, beating heart clinging on to life.

The square was now completely empty. The boules players had gathered in a little smoky café and were chatting with the fairground people. Their life seemed simple and untroubled.

"But still, you know, it's going to be a challenge to pretend there's nothing the matter..."

As I said this, something occurred to me.

"So in that case," I said, "when you gave me the

maths answers at the beginning of term, you were already thinking ... I mean, it was so that I would help you when you couldn't see any more?"

"Not to start with. I gave you the answers because there was something about you that amused me, something a bit old-fashioned. You remind me a bit of—"

"Clark Gable, I know. I've got the vintage touch. And then what happened?"

"Stop looking at me like that, for heaven's sake... What happened then was that I realized you were resourceful. And generous. And sensitive. And I felt sure that you would help me and not let me down. Then I fell in love with you and stopped thinking about anything at all."

I wondered if I'd heard right and if this was the end of exile. I nearly asked her to repeat it, but since she was blushing a bit, it seemed best to say nothing. I stared at the bunch of flowers, wondering what their names were, with my heart exploding into little pieces. For no particular reason, I began to count the petals. Then we looked at the clouds for a while. All I wanted to do was to run away as fast as possible without looking back. I don't know why, but I found myself remembering the TV programme about concentration camps that I'd watched with Dad.

Marie's determined voice broke into my thoughts.

"OK, let's sum up the situation. Firstly, in a few days' time, or at the latest after the Christmas holidays, it's going to be curtains…"

"Like Helen Keller?" I butted in, wanting to make a cultural reference.

"Like Helen Keller, exactly. Although I can still hear. Secondly, I need your help to stop anyone noticing at school. My marks mustn't drop, because the music school only accepts brainy people. But I can't do it on my own, so you'll have to be like Ariadne's thread and lead me through the labyrinth. Thirdly, why don't we go to the funfair together tomorrow? Now let's go and have lunch. Mum's made lasagne and an awesome dessert."

Marie showed me into a huge living room, flooded with light from tall bay windows. Her mother came in and I held out my bouquet. She buried her nose in it.

"There's no point in doing that, Madame, they're made from fabric. I thought they would last longer. And also that they would be more elegant."

"You were quite right," she said, ushering us towards a table laden with lots of appetizing little nibbles.

Marie's father joined us at the table. He was dressed like a duke and he crossed his legs in a very posh way.

"So, Victor, you're in the same class as Marie, I believe?"

"Yes, that's right, in the same class though not in the same league."

They smiled and that was a good start. I bit into something small and round. It was very hard.

"Excuse me, Victor, I think you need to take it out of the shell first," explained Marie's mother, very kindly, handing me some special tweezers.

"Do you enjoy your schoolwork?" Marie's father asked me.

I thought for a moment. Marie's parents were smiling at me in a very friendly way. I noticed that Marie's lips were just like her mother's.

"I've got nothing against it, if you know what I mean. It's schoolwork that's got something against me."

"Did you know that Einstein only began speaking when he was five and before then everyone thought he had learning difficulties?"

"He was lucky. In my case, that was just the age that I began to have difficulties. Before then, everyone left me in peace."

Marie's mother went back and forth to the kitchen. She walked in a graceful, refined way. What a supersonically stylish environment. *If you could see me now, Dad,* I said to myself, *you wouldn't believe it!*

"Are you a musician too, perhaps?" asked Marie's father.

"Not at all, Monsieur. I've never been able to tell the difference between a symphony and a car crash. My father paid for me to have piano lessons when I was younger, and frankly, if you want my opinion, it was money down the drain."

"Victor says that, but actually..." Marie interrupted.

My ears began to ring. She was looking at me. I shut my eyes and held my breath, as if I was facing a firing squad.

"... He's a real music lover. He knows how to listen properly and he makes very sensitive judgements."

I turned scarlet, partly because of my secret about The Rattletraps, but mostly because of the compliment.

"Do you know that at the end of the year our daughter's going to audition for a very prestigious music school? We're very happy for her, it's going to be a turning point in her life, isn't that so, Marie?"

She smiled at her father and then looked straight

at me. It was as though we were bound together by the secret we shared.

"It'll be ready in five minutes," said Marie's mother, sitting back down again.

Just as well, I thought. The lasagne would give me confidence. I always need to fill my belly before I can relax.

On the table, around the plates, there was so much cutlery that it looked as though the knives and forks had been busy making babies. There were pink napkins in the glasses, folded in the shape of birds with their wings spread open. I was impressed by how elegant it all was.

I didn't want them to think me a slob, so I didn't ask about the array of cutlery. Frankly, just one fork would have been more than enough for me. So while trying to follow the conversation, I kept a watchful eye on Marie and attempted to use the cutlery like she did, in the same order. It was a bit complicated, especially for the starter, which was a kind of wobbly savoury mousse that you had to pick up with a big spoon, helped along by a smaller spoon, and then grab with a sort of tapered spatula. I found it as difficult as managing my compass in maths: it always slid away at the last moment too.

Marie's mother put the dish of lasagne down on the table.

"And what's your favourite subject at school?" she asked, as she took my plate.

"Oh, you know … it depends!"

"What does it depend on?" she wanted to know as she handed me back my plate, which now looked as though it had the whole of Italy piled on it.

"On which day it is. Yes, it depends on which day it is. On the whole, I like art best."

This came to me out of the blue, like a brainwave, because of the room's artistic decor.

"Abstract art?"

I've never really understood this word. Precisely because it's too abstract.

"Of course," I said. "It's the most beautiful kind."

Then I was able to relax for a few moments, because they began to talk to each other about modern art exhibitions taking place in London and Paris. I wondered what Dad was doing, and I imagined him with his nose under the Panhard's bonnet and his hands all oily. He was probably balancing his sandwich on the carburettor so as not to waste any time. Then I tried to get a handle on the conversation again. I no longer had any idea what they were on

172

about and it reminded me of the way I dipped in and out of some lessons at school.

Then, while waiting for dessert, we settled down on a sofa and leafed through some exhibition catalogues, showing paintings covered in multi-coloured crosses. After looking at them for a while, I actually began to find them quite interesting.

"All things considered," I observed, "I find that if you look at something long enough it becomes interesting."

"Hah! Flaubert!" said Marie's father, absent-mindedly.

"What?"

"It was Flaubert, the writer, who said that. About a tree, I think."

I'd always thought that Flaubert was a journalist. I couldn't get it out of my head, since it was my dear uncle Zak who once told me so.

Still, it's funny to think that it's possible to have the same ideas as people who are famous for being seriously brainy. It's an odd thing: it's hard to tell if it makes you feel bigger or them seem smaller. But I was beginning to feel confident now, so I carried on sharing my views on aesthetics.

"It's true, you know. See these little crosses. Well,

if you look at them long enough, they make a picture of a woman in the bath."

"Do you think so?" said Marie's father, who was now really interested. "A woman in the bath ... really?"

He started turning the book round and round.

"Yes! Look, you can see the arms and the neck clearly here, and there are the boo— you know, the whatsits ... the things for feeding babies... There's the edge of the bath... You can even see the soap... See? It's as clear as anything!"

All three of them looked at me as though I was some sort of weird insect.

"What about the title?" asked Marie.

"The title? What title?"

"Here, look: Monochrome Factory."

I sighed. I wasn't going to make an issue about the word "monochrome", because vocabulary like that is just way out of reach.

"It's only a very small title. And anyway a title doesn't mean much. Think of The Three Musketeers, well, there were four of them! So, yeah. And that's not even modern art. So it goes to show, with what's produced these days, nobody's going to give a stuff about titles..."

"Mind you, he's got a point," said Marie's mother. "It's the same sort of thing with music. In the old days you used to get the 'Seventh Symphony', which tells you exactly what it means: after the Sixth and before the Eighth. Whereas nowadays…"

Encouraged by this, I thought I'd throw in a comparison between modern painting and the Asterix books, but it was obvious they hadn't read any of them, even if they did try to cover it up.

The conversation rolled on pleasantly for a while. My confidence kept growing. I felt good and I began to see that Panhard cars might not be the only interesting things in the world. It went a bit pear-shaped in the end because I lacked relevant facts. Marie's father suddenly asked me, "Do you like Pollock?"

Pollock – why was he talking about fish? At first, I wondered whether he was making fun of me because of my limitations, but I often get that impression, so maybe not… Then I came to the conclusion that he must have a second job as a fishmonger. Being the ear of an auction perhaps didn't bring enough in, financially speaking.

As I hesitated, he told me that the previous week he'd sold a whole load of Pollocks and he'd felt sickened by it. I couldn't see why: it wasn't as though he'd had to eat them.

"Can you believe it, one went to Berlin for three million."

A pollock for three million! Was that some kind of a boast?

"Was it a whopper?" I asked tentatively.

It seemed a ridiculous price. Marie was frowning. She appeared to be mesmerized. And then all of a sudden she burst out laughing. I wiped my sleeve across my moustache, just in case...

"No, not at all, no more than thirty centimetres by thirty! It was just a small Pollock!" said her father.

A square pollock for three million, this was beginning to seem a little fishy to me. Marie was still laughing. I discreetly checked my flies, but no, they weren't undone.

"Personally, I like the black and white Pollocks best," said Marie's father.

"That's a variety I've never tried! Do you cook them the same way?"

Marie leant towards me and whispered in my ear. I pretended to take no notice.

How could I have known that Pollock, first name Jackson, was a painter? What kind of a name is that?

Mr Pollock... I wanted to laugh, but I managed to keep a straight face. At last Marie's mother ceremoniously brought in the dessert, in a big bowl. It was another Italian dish, and it deserved a compliment.

"Wow! Kamasutra! Thank you, that's one of my favourite desserts!"

I held out my plate, with a massive smile of appreciation.

They were totally bewildered. There was no doubt about that: I was watching them out of the corner of my eye.

"Ka— what did you say?" asked Marie, speaking slowly and clearly.

"You know, kamasutra, the Italian dessert, of course. Are we going to eat it or send it off to a museum?"

"OK, I've got it," said Marie's father. "Do you mean tiramisu?"

"Exactly," I confirmed. "Tiramisu."

There was a pause for reflection. The atmosphere was exceptionally exquisite.

On the whole, I think I made an excellent impression.

All the same, my night ended with a really toxic nightmare. I was fishing in a very calm river.

Suddenly, there was something pulling on the end of my line. So I reeled it in as hard as I could and at last I hauled a sort of floppy, slimy catfish out of the water and onto the vivid green grass. It had a menacing expression that left me with an uncomfortable feeling when I woke up. Yet there wasn't anything particularly to fear about the day ahead: I was going to meet Marie at the funfair in front of the ticket booth for the Haunted House, and later the Metro were coming for a rehearsal, to put the final touches to the concert they refused to give up on. Dad was a bit disappointed because the day before he'd fine-tuned the Panhard to within an inch of its life, so that he could take part in a meet for cars that are on the verge of extinction. He'd been hoping to take me along, but he understood that for once I had other priorities. So he advised me to go and have a shave.

As I made my way to the fair, I thought about how I could possibly get out of the concert. Of course, I was still a fan of rock music, with its hyperactive freaks thrashing around and blasting out their massive decibels. But it was difficult to ignore the fact that it was not in the same league as the delicate, purposeful music that Marie played, reading the notes better than I could read words.

When I saw Marie in front of the Haunted House, I thought I'd better stop thinking about all this before it ruined my afternoon. Anyway, when you're thirteen, things tend to sort themselves out in the end.

We wandered around the stalls and without thinking I suggested sharing a toffee apple. As soon as I'd said it I turned as red as the apple itself. She gave me a funny look and then our noses touched as we each took a bite into opposite sides.

"You've got a red moustache," she said.

"So have you."

We burst out laughing and went into a big glass maze, still with our moustaches. You had to be really careful, or you banged your nose against the transparent panels. There were some kids bawling because they'd lost their parents: they could see them but couldn't find a way of getting to them. It was as though they were learning about exile for the first time. Perhaps it wasn't that different from life: there you are, endlessly tormented as you circle around each other, trying to touch without ever getting close. Marie and I concentrated hard as we weaved around the maze together. But there came a point when I looked back and realized she was no longer following me. There was nothing but emptiness, which is a disorientating feeling.

Marie was actually a few metres behind me, helping a little kid to get up. She was wiping his nose with a tissue all splattered with blood. I was reminded of my blackbird. Then the mother turned up and took the kid away in her arms, sounding off about the maze being a load of rubbish and whose idea was it to invent something so stupid? After that, Marie and I tried to get back together, but we made the mistake of both moving at the same time, so that we kept going past each other. It really felt like we were getting close, and then at the last moment we'd find ourselves separated by an invisible wall. At first, it made us laugh, but after a while not so much – in fact we started to panic. I tried to keep still and guide her from a distance, and then we tried it the other way round, but nothing was working. We couldn't find a way of reaching each other. It was as though we'd lost every possibility of guiding, helping or even understanding one another. We ended up in a blind alley, separated by a plexiglass panel. There was a wide, desperate sort of smile on Marie's face. Was this real or was I dreaming? I couldn't tell any more. She put her hands on the panel with her fingers spread out, and I put mine against hers. It was as though we'd both been pinned there, face to face, on either side of the glass. We stayed like that for some time gazing at each other: we found it impossible to draw apart, as though we were looking at ourselves in a mirror. Eventually we got back together outside. The sun was shining and you could smell the candyfloss. We went on the bumper cars and Marie wanted to drive.

"You see, this could be the last time I'm able to do anything like this…"

Everyone seemed to be watching us and I was happy because I thought our car had more style than any of the others. Several minutes went by before I realized that Marie was driving with her eyes closed. It really wasn't going to be easy getting her to the end of the year without anyone noticing something was wrong. I almost brought the subject up, but then I chickened out.

Afterwards we walked through the fair, still unsteady on our feet from the ride. The lights from the carousels merged with the Christmas fairy lights. It was cold, and our breath came out in little frosty clouds. Suddenly, Marie stopped dead and squeezed my arm hard.

"Why don't we go on the ghost train!"

She really seemed to enjoy the idea that we'd be scared together. I didn't have the heart to refuse and I tried to look very chilled about it, but the truth is I couldn't shake off sad thoughts that troubled me far more than all the ghosts in the world. I kept imagining Marie left all alone with her little suitcase in a specialist college for the blind – waving goodbye with no one there. I absolutely had to ask Haisam for advice: he was the only one who could help me see the whole thing more clearly. Then I stopped turning all this around in my mind, because the fluorescent skeletons were rearing up in front of us, wailing so alarmingly that Marie squeezed tightly up against me. I could feel her hair tickling my cheek. It was a good thing I'd remembered to shave. Then our car stopped for quite a long time. We could hear mournful sounds in the dark.

"I'm frightened of ghosts!" whispered Marie.

I had no time to answer because I could feel her mouth against mine. And she pressed so hard it felt like being gagged. I could feel her tongue swivelling about in all directions like a crank handle. I wanted to explode with laughter, but it seemed best to hold back. Just then, our car set off again and it was goodbye to the ghosts. We moved apart and went out into the light. We both felt slightly awkward, for obvious reasons. She was very pensive: I was sure she must be regretting it.

"You seem sad," I said.

"No, not at all. It's just that I wonder if we did it quite right. Last week, at the dentist, I read the instructions in a magazine, and I'm pretty sure it was right. But you know how it is with instruction manuals, everything always ends up back to front..."

"No. That was definitely the right way. In theory, at any rate."

"And in practice?"

"I've no idea, I only knew the theory."

We hurried off in different directions, because Marie had to practise her cello and I was already late for the rehearsal with Etienne and Marcel. It was funny, because we said goodbye quite formally. Intimacy is a complicated business. I didn't mind leaving her when things had gone so well between us: in a way I was anxious to think it all over. And that's something you can only do on your own, as Dad has often told me.

No one was at home, neither Dad nor Etienne and Marcel. Nor the Panhard. The place was deserted.

I went up to my room under the roof and sat down at my desk. I was in the mood for meditation, which is *the action of reflecting deeply and at length upon a subject*. It's something that never does any harm, in my opinion. My dear Egyptian was often a "Nile crocodile" and the meditative approach seemed to work pretty well for him, so it felt reassuring to follow his example. My first concern was how to get out of The Rattletraps' concert without looking like a quitter and without wounding the Metro's pride, and my second was whether I was up to helping Marie. Two big problems.

I heard the Panhard engine and then voices in the yard. Through the window I saw that Etienne and Marcel had come back with Dad, who'd taken them for a spin. I went down to join them. I could see straight away that something wasn't right. Etienne gave me the news.

"It sucks at home!"

"Why?"

"It's divorce."

I looked puzzled, so Marcel explained, "He means our parents are divorcing. They've been yelling at each other all day long. I thought they were going to tear each others' guts out. They can't agree on what should happen. They're going to court about our custody."

"They can't cut you in half. It's impossible to cut a Metro station in half. There was a king like that once, who wanted to cut children in half and divvy them up, but I can't remember his name."

"It's funny, though," said Etienne. "I'd never have thought it was something they'd fight so hard about!"

He seemed deep in thought.

"It's to be expected," I pointed out. "All parents fight to keep their children with them. Well, almost all…"

The memory of my mother flitted across my mind. They stared at me wide-eyed.

"No, that's not it at all. It's the other way round. They're so fed up with us that neither of them wants to keep us. So Mum's taking Dad to court to make him take us, and Dad's doing the opposite. They both want to prove that the other one would take better care of us. Dad's bound to tell the judge that he beats us and Mum will probably say she makes us cook and clean while she has a wild time out clubbing."

"That's unusual," I said. "Dad and I watched a TV programme about divorce the other day, but they didn't mention that scenario."

They seemed distracted – they weren't themselves at all. It wasn't a good day to talk to them about my decision regarding the concert. We began to play. I scratched at my guitar and shouted into the mike, but without much conviction:

"Don't drive us crazy
This work it just ain't easy
We feel like being lazy
Don't drive us crazy
To hell with being busy
We're so mad it makes us dizzy."

"Your lyrics are really cool, especially the rhymes," said Etienne, as if he was the expert.

He was just flattering me. I'd written the words when I was a revolutionary, and revolution sometimes makes you do or think things that later on mean nothing to you at all.

Marcel went one further.

"You should show them to the English teacher. I'm sure she'd read them out loud to the whole class. It's like … you know who I mean…"

He wanted to compare me to a writer we'd studied in English.

"It's like William Worthwords, that's what it is."

So then I said, "Don't you think it's really just a racket, our music?"

I realized straight away that I'd gone too far. They looked at each other and I thought they were going to vaporize. So I back-pedalled and as per usual I said the first thing that came into my head.

"No, I was joking! Anyway, having an instinct for it is all that counts!"

"What instinct?" asked Marcel, who understood nothing about symbolic imagery.

"It's an expression," said Etienne. "He means poetic instinct: when you have a passion for music, who gives a monkey's about reading the notes! Isn't that right?"

The great thing about saying any old rubbish to worm your way out of trouble is that there's always someone around who'll get the wrong end of the stick.

"Yes, that's it!" I said, to put an end to it.

Compassion is a real pain, because it makes you talk nonsense. I thought about Marie, who would be having her music lesson, and all the years it took her to learn to play her instrument. Poetic and musical passion mostly come from hard graft, but how could

187

I have explained that to Etienne and Marcel? Then we changed the subject, because Etienne had been to see the careers advisor about a new professional direction he wanted to take. He'd explained to her that he'd given up on the idea of being a chicken breast cutter and now wanted to be a proctologist. But she didn't know what that was, so he'd explained that it was a doctor specializing in the anus. Well, of course, she thought he was making a fool out of her, so she blew her top. Then she wound up Lucky Luke, who gave him hours of detention and threatened to cancel the concert.

"Personally," said Etienne, "I think that sort of attitude doesn't encourage professional development."

In the evening, I was puzzling over the word, so I looked it up in my dictionary:

Proctologist *specialist in proctology.*

Since that didn't get me very far, I looked up "proctology".

Proctology *the branch of medicine that deals with diseases of the anus and rectum.*

A job like that was bound to need many years of study, a bit like a dentist. Well, now I knew. I went downstairs to see Dad, who'd turned on the TV and was watching a film called *Paris in the Month of August*, with Charles Aznavour in the lead role. I really liked it, the plot was very entertaining. It was about an ordinary, unremarkable man, who worked in the fishing equipment section of a department store. While his wife was away on holiday, he fell in love with a very beautiful young English model who was working in Paris. He wanted to spend as much time with her as possible and take advantage of the way moral standards were becoming more relaxed. So in order to get sick leave from work, he had the bright idea of sticking a fish hook deep into his hand. Problem solved, just like that. An excellent film all round, in fact, and very moving too.

Dad was fascinated by the film. I don't know if it was the empty city flooded in sunlight or the love story between the man and the model that enthralled him, but he seemed to be trying to hypnotize the television: he was almost licking the screen. Anyway, the film gave me an idea and although it was slightly hazy at first, I'd got it all worked out by the next morning. At dawn, I was down in the cellar hunting around for Dad's fishing equipment. The size twelve hook looked enormous to me, plus it was covered in rust. I made myself think of *Paris in the Month of August* and Aznavour with the fish hook stuck in his hand. It was in a good cause: I was really doing this for Marie, so that she wouldn't have to hear me braying at the concert and wouldn't be disappointed in me. It's all very well to be a figure of fun, but once you've learnt to see things in a slightly more dignified and high-minded way, you get fed up with it, that's all I can say.

I closed my eyes and stuck the hook into my left hand. I screamed out loud, my eyes dimmed and luckily Dad turned up just in time to catch me before I crashed to the floor. He wrapped my hand in a big cloth that kept getting redder and redder as we drove in the Panhard to the hospital. There were Christmas decorations in the A&E department and a big Father Christmas who seemed to be watching over the patients.

While we were waiting, Dad said, "I still can't work out what you were doing trying to fish for your own hand in the cellar at dawn..."

To shut him up, I gave a couple of extra groans.

"Now you remind me of that big pike I caught in

the Loire twenty years ago," he said.

"Dad," I said, "Don't worry, Dad, I did it for love, which is the end of being exiled from oneself…"

I felt his hand on my head, and I knew he understood. And then I passed out.

8

When Haisam asked me, on the first morning back at school after the Christmas holidays, why I had a big bandage around my hand, I was tempted to tell him everything – the whole truth – and to ask his advice about helping Marie. But in the end I just told him I'd trapped my hand in the bonnet of the Panhard. He gave me an odd look, as though to say: *why are you lying to me, since you know there's no point?* He was playing chess with his father and every now and then they would toss out bizarre terms that still meant absolutely nothing to me: the East Indian Defence, the Nimzo-Indian Defence, the Rubinstein Attack, the Sämisch Variation, the Spielmann Variation, the Sicilian Defence. For the first time, I was beginning to hate the game: it seemed as complicated and nerve-racking as the world itself. School was also beginning to feel like a big chessboard full of traps, which Marie and I would have to struggle across, just as we'd struggled to get through the maze at the fair. For the last few days I'd had a knot in my stomach and it had been getting tighter as the end of the holidays approached. As for Haisam, his father had given him a book of theory for Christmas, all about the "hypermodern revolution in chess". But I think my anxiety about Marie meant that I no longer admired his freakish intelligence quite so much.

The game finished and we began to munch Turkish delight. Haisam's father started telling us about Istanbul, the city of his birth, and its attractions: the Golden Horn, the Bosphorus, the Galata Bridge and all that stuff. It wasn't really the best time to be reminiscing, because all the kids were pouring into school, although that didn't seem to bother him much. In general I was a bit wary of putting questions to my noble Egyptian's Turkish father, but on that day I did ask him whether he ever felt like going back to his roots.

"Turkey isn't Turkey any more... It's a shadow of its former self. It's sad, but that's the way it is! There's nothing to be done but dream about its glorious history…"

I could see that he was feeling melancholic about his ancestral lands and I too began to daydream, lulled by all those strange names he kept mentioning: Istanbul … Kassim Pasha … the Galata Bridge … the famous Princes' Islands, where he'd lived as a child and which he was clearly trying to recreate in his lodge, on a smaller scale.

The bell rang and that brought me back down to earth.

I looked out for Marie, feeling desperately anxious. I bumped into Marcel and Etienne, who were on their way to a different class. I'd honestly thought that they would be in a strop with me for ever and would never speak to me again, but in fact they just asked me how my hand was. The cancellation of the concert hadn't bothered them too much, because around that time their father had tried to strangle their mother with a string from Etienne's bass guitar and in self-defence their mother had broken Marcel's drumsticks over her husband's head. It was all-out war, and the atmosphere was post-nuclear.

In class, I noticed that the maths teacher was

looking really pretty, with a bow in her hair, which showed she was taking a new interest in her personal appearance. She still limped, but you didn't notice it so much because her face was nicer to look at. Marie wasn't there, and the worst possible thoughts went through my mind. Perhaps they'd already put her, against her will, in the special college for the blind.

The teacher wished us a happy new year, and said she hoped that it would bring us everything we wanted. For the first time ever, those words actually meant something specific to me. Marie still hadn't arrived and I was getting seriously worried. We made a start on an exercise. It was a right pain in the backside:

Multiply out and simplify:
$$A = 3(x + 1) + (x + 2)(x - 3).$$

I couldn't get my head around it. I will always wonder why mathematicians are so obsessed with multiplying out if they then want to go straight ahead and simplify. I mean, get real.

We all had our heads down, when there was a knock on the door and Marie came in. And yes, I could see straight away that something had changed.

She apologized for being late and took three careful steps to the teacher's desk to hand in a late note, planting her feet flat on the floor, a bit like an astronaut. She looked as though she was staring, but I knew that her eyes were empty. Watching her feet, I could see that she was concentrating on taking very regular steps. She sat down calmly and got her things out in the normal way, except there was nothing normal about it. I didn't know what to say to her and her composure put the wind up me — a radioactive wind, that's what I thought at the time. While the others were slogging away, she whispered to me, "Quick, tell me what we're supposed to do."

"Multiply out and simplify: $A = 3(x + 1) + (x + 2)(x - 3)$" I muttered as quietly as possible.

"OK. Get on with your work."

I could see she was really concentrating: her lips were moving slightly. Then she tried to write on a sheet of paper, but her writing was going all over the place, up, down, zigzagging like a roller coaster, a real arithmetic big dipper. What with her staring eyes and her jumbled handwriting, she was going to get caught out on the first day, or at least raise serious suspicions. The teacher began to hobble between the desks, still weighed down by her dead baby. A dead child is surprisingly heavy, especially when you have to carry it around all the time. I realized she was going to see Marie's haphazard writing, so quick as lightning I grabbed the paper from her and put it down on the desk in front of me. As the teacher reached my desk, everyone looked at me. I held the paper out to her.

"Here's the answer," I said confidently. "It's very badly written but I think it's right."

"Yes, it's right, but why is it such a horrible mess?"

My brain went into overdrive and this is what came out.

"It's because of the passion..."

"The passion?"

"Mathematical passion. An intense feeling: like an instinct. The same phenomenon has often been observed with poetry and music."

I looked her straight in the eye. Boldly saying the first thing that comes into your head is often the best way out of a tricky situation. She didn't quite know how to respond and Marie created a diversion by offering to give the answer to the whole class.

"$A = 3(x + 1) + (x + 2)(x - 3)$. Therefore $A = 3x + 3 + x^2 - 3x + 2x - 6 = x^2 + 2x - 3$."

I was completely astonished, because she'd pulled

that out of nowhere with nothing to cling on to except the trapeze of her intelligence and her memory. How pathetic I was in comparison. While all the others were scrabbling to put away their things, Marie leant casually towards me and whispered, "Walk in front of me to clear my way through. Don't go too far ahead, I'm still not very good at getting my bearings. Try to stamp your feet a bit so that I don't lose the thread…"

Her face twisted in a wretched smile. As we made our way along the corridors, I stamped my feet like a flamenco dancer. Van Gogh, still with a piece of sticking plaster on his ear, said as he passed by, "Hey, did you go to Spain for the holidays?"

But I didn't want to stoop to his level, so I simply told him he was a mug. He said I was a mug too, but I was ready for that and came straight back with, "You're so full of it, you've got to be the biggest mug of all."

I don't know why, but this retort shuts them up every time. It's quite something.

Marie and I reached the playground and I left her there, just like a towplane releasing a glider. I watched her walk steadily off. Her lips were moving very slightly and I realized she was counting her steps. She must have done the same thing when she gave her note to the teacher and got back to her own desk. The very thought of it nearly made me keel over in admiration, with tears in my eyes. Well, I'm exaggerating a bit, but you can't blame me.

After school, on the way home, she confirmed it: she'd been calculating distances for weeks, and now they were all recorded in her brain. She'd turned the school into an immense geometrical plane, divided up into carefully measured squares.

"For instance, you see, it's twelve steps from your Egyptian friend's lodge to the lockers. From the school gates to Lucky Luke's office it's twenty-eight steps if you go on the right-hand side, thirty-seven if you go on the left. From the toilets to the canteen it's seventy-eight steps, unless they've put up display panels for an exhibition, in which case you have to go round them, making a hundred and seventeen steps."

We walked on towards the village. I was amazed because Marie seemed to know where she was going. I even wondered for a moment if she was having me on about going blind, but then I felt really guilty. And in any case, just when I was looking the other way and didn't have time to react, I heard a noise like someone banging a gong: I turned to see her on the ground beside the postbox she'd crashed into. She was rubbing her forehead, where a big red lump was forming, with a bleak look on her face. I could see how despondent she was. She seemed so strong and proud, even more so since she'd been hiding her disability, but all this was a huge deal in terms of her dignity. In actual fact she was like everyone else: lost and all alone in her misfortune. She was trying not to cry. It was odd to see translucent tears forming in those eyes that could no longer see.

I leant towards her and she gripped hold of my arm. I could lift her weight quite easily, just like my poor weak little blackbird. When I think back to that scene it unfolds as though in slow motion. She got to her feet and we continued on our way in silence. She kept a gentle hold on my arm, and I wasn't sure whether I hoped someone we knew would see us, or whether I dreaded the possibility. I'd often observed old couples taking a walk together just as we were doing, and being tethered to her like that gave me the sense of being more firmly rooted to the earth. I didn't feel at all blurry any more. It was exactly like Dad's theory about love and the end of exile. I looked at her out of the corner of my eye, because I had the feeling she'd know she was being watched unless I was discreet about it. I'd heard on the radio that blind people have a lot of intuition. I'd even looked it up in the dictionary.

Intuition *an ability to understand something immediately, without conscious reasoning. An instinctive feeling, more or less precise, about something that cannot be verified or that has not yet happened.*

It's a handy thing, intuition, it has a lot of uses.

When we were in sight of the church, she asked, "What did you do to your left hand? What's that bandage?"

"I fished myself."

"You fished yourself?"

She turned towards me. Her eyes were staring straight into mine. There was nothing funny about it. It was hard to know what to do – I had no instruction manual for looking into blind eyes.

"Yes, well, I stuck a size twelve fish hook into my hand while I was rummaging through Dad's fishing equipment. Then I got all tangled up in the line and reeled myself in. I'll tell you what, I wouldn't like to be a pike."

I was looking between her eyes, just above her

nose, which felt less awkward than looking into her eyes or in a completely different direction. And then I was astounded, because she said, "Yes, I know, don't worry, it's really hard to look a blind person in the eyes... Just do what you can. If you like, I can stop looking at you when we're talking."

"Looking at me? But it's me who's looking at you!"

"That's what you think, because you don't get it, but I am looking at you. Do you want me to stop?"

She must have been speaking from intuition, that useful ability to understand without conscious reasoning. So what on earth was I supposed to say?

"No, I'd prefer you to go on looking at me... I like it when you look at me..."

Sometimes you only realize things are true after you've said them. She smiled and it occurred to me that eyes aren't the only way to see. Little by little, you do eventually come to understand some very important things in life. It's hard to believe, because you couldn't care less about them to start with. Slowly but surely, that's how you become less small.

The people from the fair had left and the boules players were back in the square. Now and then you could hear the metal balls knocking against each other.

"Shall we go into the church?" asked Marie.

I thought back to the first time I'd shot into that little church. In four months, I'd now been to church more often than in the last twelve years. It was dark and cold inside. Churches aren't very welcoming places if you're looking for consolation. Comfort is important for that: it's no joke if you have to put up with even more suffering before you can be consoled. I know you shouldn't be too self-indulgent, but still.

In the church, it was now Marie who was leading me, not the other way around. Anyone would have thought that she was able to see perfectly and that I was the blind one. We stopped in front of a statue of the Virgin Mary holding her son, all broken from the crucifixion. I've never really liked that sort of religious stuff: speaking bluntly, all that business with the cross, I don't really get it, to be honest. But in the current situation, I was keen to take an interest and show that I was open to spiritual things. Marie was murmuring in front of the statue and I assumed she was praying.

Then she leant towards me and asked, "Do you believe in miracles?"

I was stuck for a reply, I can tell you.

"It depends…" I said, hesitantly.

"It depends on what?"

"Oh … it depends … it depends … well, it depends on the miracle!"

There was nothing more to say after that. But before leaving her in front of her big square house, I told her not to forget the money for the school trip to Paris. Our art teacher wanted to take us to the Louvre Museum in the spring. Marie pressed her lips together and I could see she was worried, because paintings aren't the same as maths: it's a lot more complicated when you can't see anything at all. I told her I'd give some thought to the problem. Then we said goodbye and I watched her going a little stiffly up the garden path, probably focused on counting her steps. That was her life now: a life counted out in footsteps.

I ran home. Dad was fumbling about with the Panhard's engine. He asked if I wanted to help him, but I said I'd got work to do. I could see he was trying to hold back a smile. All the same, I suggested that he should check the spring-drive turbine fan, because it seemed to me that the Aerodyne motor was badly overheating. I had a snack and then I leant out of the window and asked him, "Hey, Dad, do you know what paintings there are at the Louvre?"

He looked up, holding an 18 mm spanner.

"The Mona Lisa. That's what there is at the Louvre. It's by Leonardo da Vinci, an Italian painter."

I was lucky to have such a seriously cultured father.

In my bedroom, I got out my art things. I laid the tubes of paint out neatly on my table. A lot of them were squashed flat. They looked like a colony of multi-coloured slugs. I found a picture of the Mona Lisa in Dad's encyclopaedia and I also learnt that the lady in the picture was known for her serene and enigmatic smile. I had a look in my dictionary:

Serene *calm, peaceful; having a tranquillity that comes from an untroubled conscience.*

Enigmatic *difficult to understand or interpret; mysterious.*

Nothing could have reminded me more of my dear Egyptian. So I set to work with a warm and friendly feeling for the Mona Lisa.

Late in the evening, Dad came up to say goodnight. I showed him my painting.

"Do you see what it is?"

"Of course."

I smiled. I felt relieved and really quite pleased with myself. Almost certainly, at the museum, we'd be asked to copy the *Mona Lisa*, the most famous painting there. If we ran into difficulties, all I'd need to do would be to slip Marie my copy.

"Of course I see what it is. It's a lovely plate of steaming spaghetti, with a little dish of Parmesan cheese right beside it."

9

There are times when life can be really tough. It didn't take long for me to figure that out. It's responsibility that causes the most trouble and anxiety. There are no two ways about it, when other people's problems become your own, well, that's when your life changes completely, because you've got someone who needs rescuing and you have to make a go of it. It's kind of the same with animals. For example, my poor mangled blackbird didn't weigh much, but he was a heavy responsibility, and even though he was getting his strength back I still felt anxious about him. When you're dealing with a human being it's even worse!

The most difficult thing was the handwriting, because mine was all convoluted and corkscrewed while Marie's was like her socks, without a wrinkle or a crease. She gave me some examples and I practised copying them in the evenings. Afterwards my wrist hurt as much as if I'd been playing tennis in the French Open. When we got back from school, we would get straight down to our homework. I would read out the questions and she would come up with the answers, which I had to write down in her exercise book. She was the brains and I was the brawn. While she was thinking, I gazed around her room, which was white and yellow, and very bright. All around there was silence, and outside the windows you could see the big trees in the garden swaying gently in the breeze.

After a moment or two Marie would tell me the answer in a whisper, as though she didn't want to wake me. And I would start writing. Sometimes there was a book we had to read, and then of course I had to read it to her. In the past I'd always hated reading. Everyone told me that literature could teach you loads of things, but frankly what was there to learn from these made-up stories? You could hardly tell one from another. I'd always felt that books were a bit like loaded pistols and needed to be handled with caution. Now, with Marie, things were obviously different. I don't know how to explain it, but there was something more to it: the words went in with much less trouble and when they came out again they'd somehow been transformed, for Marie. I realized that the characters in the books were her, were me, were us. In understanding their lives and their feelings, I began to understand my own life and my own feelings. So I worked my way through *The Lost Estate*, a strange novel full of mists and ponds, followed by a seventeenth-century play (acting out all the characters, including a betrayed husband and his wife Angelica, who wasn't exactly angelic). Then we read a medieval story about a knight who fights against other knights as well as a serpent and a monster, and goes completely off his head.

One day when we'd just finished one of these books, I said to Marie, "It's not so bad, literature, after all. As something to pass the time, I mean. But I find it weird that you're supposed to study it. To be honest, I can't see what there is to study in it, really I can't."

"But you know what? There are people who spend years and years writing big books called theses about the books we've read."

"And who's interested in them?"

"No one. Well, almost no one. But that's not the point, these are very clever people. They're called Doctors of Philosophy."

Well, I was learning something new every day. Even if the enterprise didn't do me any good, it wouldn't do me any harm either: everyone's entitled to choose how they spend their time. It was similar with Dad and Panhard cars. They were cars that no one bought any more. But they'd been successful in their time: Monsieur Panhard had been a pioneer of French car manufacturing at the beginning of the twentieth century. I think that's what Dad liked about them – the fact that they were on their way out and it was essential to save as many as possible so that they wouldn't be forgotten. Because the most important responsibility for human beings is to remember.

The thing we feared above all, in this business with Marie, was having to do a written assessment. Then I was in a cold sweat for three days beforehand. On the day of the damn test, I had to work really quickly, because I needed to make time to copy out my answers, imitating Marie's shipshape handwriting. I'd really made progress as a result of taking on this job, and I was even able to slip some mistakes into my work so that it wouldn't attract attention.

I could see that the maths teacher was observing my improvement with a mixture of admiration, suspicion and amusement. She often smiled at me, and I smiled back. One day, after the lesson, she gave me a funny look and said, "You're changing, Victor, you're changing..."

Without missing a beat, I replied, "You too, Miss, you're changing too. I've noticed, you have thingies in your hair, which you never had before, and your eyes are underlined in blue."

Her blushes could have generated enough heat to save the school's energy bills for at least a year. It was obvious that her romantic reactor was in meltdown. I didn't dare mention it, but I'd also spotted her limping less. It wasn't that noticeable yet, but my observation skills are second to none. I was pleased to see she was getting back on form. On TV I'd seen an oil spill that was threatening all kinds of animals and I'd told Dad that the maths teacher reminded me of those creatures stuck in the slick: she needed to be put in a de-oiling machine and then perhaps she would come out and take flight again, like the birds. He must have thought I wasn't well, because he said, "You're working too hard, I think. You're overheating."

The teacher had gone on to say that she was glad to see me doing well, and that friendship was a great support, not only at school but in life in general. Of course, she didn't know how close she was to hitting the nail on the head.

"You're right," I told her. "I'm really lucky to have a friend like Marie. Although it's also annoying, her being so good at everything, because of the humidity."

"The humidity?"

"Yes, you know, when you feel really small next to someone who's head and shoulders above you…"

"You mean humility."

Humility *the quality or state of being humble; having a low opinion of one's own importance; meekness and lack of vanity.*

"Yes, that's it. Because you know, it isn't only music she's interested in. When she has time, she reads philosophy. Before I became friends with her, I wasn't even aware such a thing existed. Did you know that the word philosophy means 'love of wisdom'?"

"No, I didn't know. You see, now you've taught me something."

Ever since Marie could no longer read, once we'd

finished our homework and planned for any hazards that might crop up the next day, she would ask me to get a philosophy book from her bookcase. Mostly they had completely baffling titles. She explained that I'd need to know about philosophy later on, and that she probably would have decided to specialize in it herself if she hadn't chosen music instead. But anyway there wasn't any choice in the matter now.

One day, wanting to impress her, I looked up some facts about the greatest philosophers. I made some notes about Plato and Aristotle and the allegory of the cave, which is a story about prisoners tied to the wall of a cave all their lives. They can only see the shadows of things moving outside and they think they're real. It's meant to tell you that knowledge isn't only about what you can see. The next day, I brought the conversation round to the subject. I wanted to trot out what I'd learnt to show her that I wasn't a buffoon, or at least not only a buffoon. But when I opened my mouth I said that in my opinion the two greatest philosophers were Arilato and Pistotle ... so then I gave up on the idea. Marie burst out laughing and said I was a genius, a real genius. I didn't know whether to be flattered or put out.

There were many things that surprised me about Marie and filled me with admiration. We were both very worried that a teacher might ask her to read something out loud. To try and avoid that, I always put up my hand to volunteer for any reading. The others could think what they liked about me, I didn't care. So I kept sticking my hand up as though my life depended on it, which it almost did. But one day the teacher wanted us to read a really difficult poem by a very young poet called Rimbaud who kept running away from home and then suddenly stopped writing and went to some place in Africa to be an arms dealer. He ended up back in France and had a leg amputated. Not the sort of thing that makes a career as a poet seem very appealing...

Anyway, to cut a long story short, the teacher asked Marie to read the poem. Disaster. It would all be over. I felt so dreadful that I could feel myself going as white as the sheet of paper on my desk, with its margins, lines, ring holes and all. What could I do? I got ready to create a diversion by falling off my chair and rolling around on the floor, throwing my dignity to the wind. But I didn't need to, because straight away, without turning a hair, Marie began to reel off the poem without tripping up once. Yet again

I wondered whether she'd been making a complete fool of me right from the start. How else could she have rattled off all those mystifying verses, without missing a beat, like a recording? Marie was brilliant at cello and loved wisdom, but surely even she couldn't do everything.

Later, in the playground, while we were waiting for lunch, I asked her if her sight was improving.

"Are you asking me that because of the poem? That's way off the mark. For a start, Arthur Rimbaud is my favourite poet. And secondly, I know hundreds of poems by heart. I was just lucky, that's all."

"But honestly, dear Marie, how on earth can you cram so much stuff inside your brain? It's ridiculous!"

She gave me a gentle smile. I think it was because of the "dear Marie". It just came out, I hadn't given it any thought. It almost felt as momentous as a marriage proposal.

"A few years ago I was ill for several months," she said. "It was when my eyes started to go wrong. I couldn't go to school, so I was able to learn lots of things. I learnt the piano too, to pass the time."

"All on your own?"

"It's not that difficult. You just have to put your fingers in the right places, that's all. And anyway, the

215

piano is only a hobby. I don't take it seriously."

"I tell you what, I'm beginning to understand why you've gone blind. It's like in a Formula One motor race: when a champion is so good that it spoils the excitement, well, they give him a handicap. So God has given you a handicap to make it fairer on other people."

"So you believe in God now, do you?"

"It's just a manner of speaking. Fate, then, if you prefer. Do you remember what the teacher said about Rimbaud being such a gifted poet? And his gangrene and his amputated leg? Well, I think that's another example of handicap. The more gifted you are, the more you pay for it. I'm not at any great risk myself, but I'm very worried about you and Haisam."

She looked at me, so to speak, with a strange expression. I could see that sometimes I said things which made her think deeply, and I found that flattering. In life, it's important to have self-esteem.

The bell rang for lunch and we headed to the canteen. It was always a tricky moment. For a start there was invariably a terrible crush on the staircase, which was dangerous for Marie. I bared my teeth and lashed out with my fists, twisting in all directions to create a protection zone around her – a kind of nature reserve for the preservation of rare species. Since everyone remembered the episode with Van Gogh, nobody tried to trespass in our territorial waters.

When we got to the counter we had to choose our meals and the pantomime that ensued was beyond a joke. It was the luck of the draw: Marie went in front of me and I watched her pile her tray high with prize-winning combinations like paté + egg mayonnaise + stew + sauerkraut. Or it was the opposite and you'd think from her selections that she was fasting as penance for something.

Sometimes she groped around, hesitated and ended up sticking her finger into a serving dish of stewed fruit, mashed potato or custard. When she got to the end of the line she looked as though she'd painted her fingers.

"Is this some special diet you're on, young lady?" teased Didier, the cook, with a smile. He watched over his canteen like an air traffic controller.

"Studying gives you an appetite," Marie said simply.

It was up to me to compensate and to restore a nutritional balance. So I adjusted my choices accordingly and my tray would either be a carbohydrate overload with mountains of mashed potato bristling with sausages or a crash diet with nothing but green, pale and stringy things. The great Didier ribbed me in his gentle way.

"So you're turning into a vegetarian?" he would ask, his hands on his hips. "You're just eating seeds and leaves these days?"

"Green things free your spirit, with all due respect."

The great Didier didn't try too hard to understand. Really he just wanted us to be well fed, however chaotically, because it was in his nature to look out for young people and see that their dietary needs were met. He was a stickler for nutrition and personally made sure we all cleared our plates. If you didn't, you got detention and had to come back after school and finish what you hadn't eaten.

When we sat down, we began trading.

"I'll swap your sauerkraut for my grated carrot, but I'm not having your veal casserole."

"Sold! as my father would say. But what's this, on this plate here in the middle?"

"Beef stew. You'll just have to do your best."

It felt like we were feeding each other, and I thought about the toffee apple we'd eaten together at the fair. Sharing food is the most intimate thing of all. The others watched, fascinated, as our forks danced from tray to tray – but they resisted any urge to comment as soon as they saw my sulphuric smile.

All the same, these sumo wrestler's meals were getting a bit much. So I took a strategic initiative and began to make loud comments as we queued up with our trays.

"Oh, what lovely beetroot! There, right in front of me, it looks absolutely delicious."

People on either side smirked a bit. But I redoubled my efforts, so that Marie would understand me.

"I didn't know carrots were in season! Did you?" I said, turning towards the people around me. "Look, I can see a tub of them just there on the right!"

Clever, huh? It was as though I was guiding Marie's hand by remote control, and the feeling it gave me made it worth being taken for a complete nutcase by the other kids. Sometimes I spoke directly to the dinner ladies, and I was impressed with my own subtle cunning.

"So, ladies," I'd bellow, "would you recommend the fish and green beans on the right or the chicken and chips on the left? Hmm? Fish on the right … or chicken on the left?"

They stared at me open-mouthed, their eyes popping.

"It's difficult ... fish on the right ... chicken on the left... I can't make up my mind..."

One day I saw one of the ladies tapping her forehead with her finger, *tap tap*, as she moved away and at that point I began to question my strategy.

But the canteen was nothing compared to the horrors of sport. We only had to hold out for a couple more months, and luckily for us in the spring term the boys and girls always did sport together. To be honest, I've never had anything against sport, but I've never had anything for it either.

When we were running round the sports ground to warm up, Marie tended to veer towards the left and off the track, and once I found her jogging along aimlessly in the middle of the football pitch. No matter how much I tried to stick close to her, she always ended up in a jam. Volleyball was even worse. She would gamely hold up her arms to show she was ready, but any ball coming towards her landed on her head, or she tried to hit it when it was already grounded. It was obvious she was totally out of sync with what was going on. It broke my heart to see her randomly hitting at thin air like that. She seemed to be battling against destiny, which never ends up exactly where you think it will either.

The worst time was when I insisted she played in goal during a game of handball. Being goalkeeper is always quite a cushy number, I thought: most of the time you don't need to do anything. I was in the middle of the court, with one eye on Marie and the other on the attackers in the opposing team, when I noticed that she was turning sideways, as though she was about to start a conversation with the goalpost. Then she turned to face in completely the opposite direction. Finally she bent her knees like a keen goalkeeper, with her hands slightly outstretched as though ready to receive the ball. She had her back to the court and was facing the net and the wall of the gym, with her bum pointing towards us. This time it seemed like we were definitely done for, so I threw everything at it. I collapsed on the ground, squealing like a piglet and holding my ankle, which caused just enough confusion to create a diversion. A little way off, Van Gogh was looking livid, bouncing the ball in a total fury. I got the feeling we were being watched very closely indeed.

At last the time came for the school trip to the Louvre Museum. Marie and I had been in training for the whole of the previous week, but I still didn't feel prepared. Marie had told me about the most famous paintings – those they might ask us to copy – and she'd given me an encyclopaedia of painting.

"You might as well tie a paintbrush to a donkey's tail!" I wailed in total despair.

"Funny you should say that," she replied. "Listen to this…"

Then she told me a story she'd heard from her father. In Paris, at the end of the nineteenth century, some artists who were fond of a drink or two had tied a paintbrush to the tail of a donkey and put a canvas behind it. And it began to paint like crazy. They put the painting into an exhibition and some very knowledgeable art critics said it was the work of a genius: they were amazed by the confident line, the original choice of colours and the sensitive execution. They thought they could picture a forest in fog or a stormy sea in the painting.

"So you see, you've got every chance of success!" said Marie.

In the museum, it was really weird to see her stand in front of paintings that none of us knew and discuss them confidently, after getting me to whisper the title to her. Anyone would have thought she could see them clearly. I had to walk right in front of her, as though we were joined invisibly by Ariadne's thread, because the Louvre is like a huge labyrinth. Since Marie had told me the story, I often thought about the myth of Ariadne. At first, I thought it was something to do with the European space launch programme, Ariane, so I didn't get the connection. But in fact that wasn't it at all: Ariadne was a young woman who fell in love with Theseus, Prince of Athens. She saved his life by giving him a ball of thread to help him find his way out of the labyrinth, the home of the terrifying Minotaur that Theseus had come to kill. I always find stories from ancient mythology reveal a lot about modern life, like a huge dictionary. It's as though everything's happened before in rough draft, to give us an idea of what to expect.

After a while, the teacher told us to sit down in a semi-circle in front of a painting and we started sketching on our drawing paper.

"What's the title, Victor? The title? How will I manage if I don't know it?" whispered Marie.

"It's too small. I can't read it."

"Right, we'll have to improvise. Describe it to me."

The teacher wandered amongst us, stroking his little goatee beard. Out of the corner of my eye

I could see Marie concentrating hard, with the end of her pink tongue sticking out. I gave her a few clues, when I could do so without being caught talking.

"On the right, there are some trees and some strangely dressed people walking about on a rock."

"And in the background?"

"In the background … a sort of river with greenery on its banks."

"And on the left?"

"Another bunch of people. The women are wearing gigantic hats. And it looks as though there's a kite floating around in the sky."

"What about the colours?"

"The sky, at the back, is almost white, apart from that it's greys and browns. And some green. I'd say it's meant to be a scout expedition. It looks as though they could be getting into boats."

"It must be *The Embarkation for Cythera*, an eighteenth-century painting."

"Did they have scouts in those days?"

"Give it a rest with your scouts!"

"And I don't see a cinema anywhere."

"Cythera, not cinema. This isn't the movies."

I got the sense that the painting must mean something, but whatever it was, it was beyond me.

I glanced at Marie's paper and it was all over the place – a real disaster. It made my heart ache to see her raising her head now and again, pretending to look at the painting. Then the teacher stopped beside her and peered at her paper. Marie must have recognized him from his footsteps, or his squeaky shoes, or perhaps from the intuition that comes with being blind.

"It's a cubist interpretation of the painting, see?" she said. "As Picasso might have done it."

The teacher scratched his chin, leaning forward slightly.

"Yes... I was just thinking to myself that I could see a hint of Picasso in your work..."

Marie and I looked at each other, well, that is, you know what I mean. I admired her nerve. In life, it's always worth giving the impression you're very sure of yourself. When you're self-confident, people tend to leave you in peace. Whereas as soon as there's the slightest crack in your confidence, it's an invitation for malice and unpleasantness of all sorts to pour in. With modern art, Marie explained on the way back, you can easily avoid the cracks. Ever since a urinal was shown in an art gallery, well, anything goes. If I'd had more facts I might have understood her point better.

When we got out of the coach that had brought us back from the museum, we all went our separate ways. Marie's father had come to fetch her and was waiting in the driving seat of a huge BMW. I thought it was second-rate compared with Dad's Panhard. It was a mild, heady spring evening and lacy clouds floated across the sky. I felt, that evening, as though I could see through time, yet life remained as mysterious as ever.

On my way home, I heard someone running after me. It was Charlotte, a girl in Year Nine who was often hanging around Van Gogh. I was pretty surprised that she was trying so hard to catch up with me. She held out an invitation to her birthday party. I asked her if Van Gogh was going to be there and if I needed to get ready to bite off his other ear.

"No, I haven't invited him. And anyway, that ear business put him in his place. So, you'll definitely come?"

"OK."

She turned on her heels and went back the way she'd come. What was I to make of this invitation? It seemed a bit fishy to me: up until then we'd never had much to do with each other. On the other hand, I have to say that over the last few months

I'd become something of a star at school, a sort of educational miracle. It was as though the guardian angel of school students had smiled upon me. So, actually, I was quite tempted to go to this party. I felt the need to see other people, to enjoy myself, to take my mind off things, because being with Marie and having all that responsibility for her was a constant worry. I was at an age when you should be able to have a good time without thinking about anything else. Yet, I couldn't help feeling a bit guilty. However much I tried to justify it to myself, I felt like a traitor to our cause. This girl, Charlotte, was not the type who'd be interested in Johann Sebastian, or the love of wisdom, or any of those high-flown things that Marie had introduced me to. But there was something in me – a sort of demon – that told me it would perhaps be fun to go and roll in a muddy ditch, because on the high peaks where my irreplaceable friend had brought me, sometimes you could feel a lack of oxygen.

I got home and Dad was watching TV. It was a history programme about the 1917 Russian Revolution.

"Did you see the *Mona Lisa*?" he asked, without taking his eyes off the screen.

227

"Yes, Dad."

"Did her eyes follow you around the room?"

"Yes, Dad, her eyes followed me around the room. She is true to her legend."

"That's good. Go and see what's in the fridge. My eyes will be following you too."

I had a snack on the corner of the table and went up to my room while the Russians were having it out with the Tsar. I stretched out on my bed and tried to imagine what Marie was doing. She must be back from her music lesson by now and was probably about to have supper. I wondered if she ever felt tempted to tell her parents everything. Then my thoughts turned towards the party the following evening. Which of the girls would be there? Adolescence, Dad had explained, is mostly a question of hormones, so I'd looked them up in my dictionary.

Hormone *a chemical substance that controls and regulates the activity of specific cells or organs.*

Well. In my case the hormones were definitely controlling a very specific organ.

It turned out that the party was taking place in a

garage, and although there was rather a peculiar atmosphere – what with the oil and the exhaust fumes – it had a certain charm. To begin with I felt uncomfortable, because I didn't know many people, but the more I was asked about my progress at school, the more at ease I felt. I relaxed and began to talk about any old thing, for instance that I'd become a fan of philosophy, which I explained means "love of wisdom". I really looked the business, because I was dressed from head to toe in a velvet suit that Dad had given me. He'd found it at the bottom of an old trunk and had been really keen to see me wear it that evening.

He'd also said, "You should go and shave."

It was the fourth time in six months, which I thought was a bit over the top, but it meant a lot to him and it didn't do me any harm.

A little entourage formed around me. I even managed to drop the names of Plato and Aristotle. One of the girls said she knew about that and I thought everything would go pear-shaped, so I breathed a sigh of relief when she said she'd seen it at the cinema and it was a really good war film.

"No, no, you're getting muddled with Platoon. The Plato I'm talking about lived in Greece in ancient times."

They wanted to know more, so I added, "He used to discuss things with Socrates in the marketplace. But eventually they had an argument so Socrates ended his life in a cave, though Plato did his best to get him out of there with some candles and shadows that made reflections on the wall."

Later, I drank some beer, because that's less complicated than philosophy. They put on some music. Some girls arrived, but the outfits they were wearing, jeez. Those girls were definitely the real thing, no way were they shadows or reflections.

Things started to go wrong when it came to the dancing. I'd just knocked back another beer when the girl who'd invited me came over and said that one of her friends really fancied me – she was keen on philosophers wearing velvet. Caught between my chemical substances and the pain in my heart when I thought of Marie, I was at a loss to know what to do. I remembered Plato and his pal Socrates. It would have been good to react like a real philosopher, in a dignified and noble manner, saying something like, "You carry on enjoying yourselves without me, I need to reflect on existential matters". And then go home to be with Dad. But it would have looked as though I was chickening out.

Once Dad and I had watched a TV programme that dealt with this very subject. It said that nowadays people have trouble separating matters of the heart from the facts of life. In the past it was much simpler, and it's the reason why couples these days can't stand the sight of each other after just a few years and split up in a storm of insults. At the time I hadn't really understood what it was all about, but now it was becoming very clear to me. So when I began to dance with the girl in question, to a very smoochy song they'd put on deliberately, I saw the problem straight away: in theory your heart and soul might be dedicated to lofty ideals, but in practice you're still pinned to the ground. This wasn't at all the end of exile, as Dad had described it, but the beginning of torment. Everything began to spin round, turning into a rush of chemical substances and specific organs and a soup of tongues.

And then there was a flash. I sprang away quickly because I immediately realized that I'd fallen into a trap. It was obvious that my dance partner had lost interest, so I tried to find out who'd taken the photograph. I asked around, but everyone looked at me as though I'd gone mad. Nobody dared say anything to my face, because people were nervous of me since I'd de-eared Van Gogh, but I did hear someone whisper, "If that's what philosophy leads to, no thanks! Leave me out of it!"

I was really worried about the photograph and thought it best to disappear as quickly as possible. Either I was going to be blackmailed, or the combination of stress and moral enlightenment would send me mad. Sometimes you can become unhinged by emotions that are too powerful.

When I got home, the Panhard seemed like a reassuring animal, sleeping with just one eye closed, and Dad was already snoring. I turned on the TV to take my mind off things, but all I could find to watch were more tragic events in history. When I'm in a normal frame of mind, I really like documentaries that teach you loads of things about what human beings are capable of. I find it instructive. I think it's good to know the worst that can happen, because then there's a better chance of nice surprises when you grow up. But that evening I was too preoccupied to concentrate on programmes like that. Then I couldn't get to sleep because I felt really guilty about Marie, and desperately anxious that my tongue kiss might make headline news.

Even without the tongue it would have been a

problem, but it wouldn't have been quite as bad. How was I going to explain myself? It's a classic scenario, I'd seen it dozens of times in films: the man gets a smack on the nose because he's been unfaithful, lied and humiliated his girl. It would be a good idea to talk to Haisam about it. As a strategic specialist, he would be able to consider it clearly and objectively. He would surely be able to advise me.

One by one the hours ticked past until Monday inevitably came around. It was one of the worst days of my life. Worse than the day when my brand-new red racing bike that Dad had brought home on the roof of the Panhard, got stolen. Worse than the days when we had courgettes for lunch at primary school. Worse than the day when I saw a completely withered plant and Dad explained that it was the same for human beings: there comes a time when there's nothing more you can do for them.

I set off early for school and waited for Haisam in the lodge. His father had once confided in me that he didn't know when his son slept. Sometimes, he would conduct an experiment: he'd put conkers in Haisam's bed and he'd find them in the same place several mornings in a row. He thought that being an insomniac was really lucky and might lead to his son becoming someone important. He used the term "majestic" to describe Haisam's abilities. "It was a majestic win," he'd said, talking about a chess game that had sealed Haisam's victory in the regional championships. That morning, Haisam's father was busy dusting the portraits of the eighteen Sultans who'd ruled the Ottoman Empire up until the eighteenth century. After that, he'd explained, Europe had carved up the Empire bit by bit, just like hunters agreeing how to divvy up their exhausted prey. And now all that remained were the leftovers.

When Haisam arrived, he looked fatter than ever. That was probably his handicap. He put the book on the hypermodern revolution in chess that his father had given him down on the table. He offered me a bowl full of Turkish delight and I watched him for a while as he chewed slowly, lost in thoughts of the Nimzo-Indian Defence and the Bayonet Attack. How on earth could I explain the situation to him? It was complicated. His father gave us a sort of very thick coffee in cups as small as thimbles. It tasted like drinking molten rubber, but I felt deeply honoured. Haisam sipped at the strange drink without ever taking his eyes off the chessboard that occupied the middle of the tiny lodge, like a centre of gravity.

"You look a bit out of sorts," he said, all of a sudden.

He must have guessed everything. You really couldn't hide anything from him: he'd probably developed intuition along with his chess skills. Just then his father gave him a bag of food for lunch.

"Hey," I said, "aren't you having lunch in the canteen?"

"No, because it's pork chops today," replied my Honourable Egyptian.

"But you had sausages last week."

"That's just how I am. Sometimes I eat kosher, sometimes I don't."

"Because sometimes you're Jewish and sometimes you're not?" I asked.

"Exactly. You've got it. Now all you need to do is learn to play chess and then you'll be really quite respectable."

I smiled. There's a certain pleasure in feeling less important than people you love and admire a lot. Just then, there was a hubbub in the playground and the sound of a murmur going through the crowd. I left Haisam because I had a nasty feeling about it, and headed towards the students' noticeboard. There was a big group of kids huddling around it.

The photos of the tongue soup from the other evening were pinned up, enlarged out of all proportion. It was Van Gogh who'd rounded everyone up. I thought the earth would swallow me, and actually that wouldn't have been a bad end right then: goodbye, world, you'll have to get along without me! Luckily, I was still concealed by the crowd and no one had noticed me. I put the collar of my jacket up as I waited to see what would happen next, scanning the faces for Marie. I had to find her before some well-intentioned person brought her up to speed. I felt a sort of groundswell behind me: it was Haisam. Perhaps not everything was lost after all.

"This is going to hit the fan!" I said, from deep down inside my jacket. The collar was pulled up to my ears.

He put his great paw on my shoulder, in that comforting way of his.

"It does you good to feel shame once in a while."

I came across it later in the dictionary:

Shame *humiliation caused by the consciousness of dishonourable behaviour. See abjection, unworthiness, disgrace, ignominy.*

Judging by the number of synonyms, it must be quite a common experience.

"Maybe it will do me good one day, but for the moment it's checkmate, over and done with."

He smiled. I think he still had a piece of Turkish delight in his mouth.

"Not yet. The Nimzo-Indian Defence is exceptionally versatile. It's useful for undermining your opponent's strategy. The defence consists of rigorously demonstrating to your opponent that you have a full grasp of the complexity of your situation, which outweighs any traps that may have been set for you."

From the depths of my jacket, as if from the depths of Plato's cave, I wondered whether he was going mad, with his mania for impenetrable language. Much later – really a long time later, once he'd become a great chess champion, and I was watching him on TV, about a thousand moves ahead of everyone else – I often thought that he still had that same air of madness about him.

"What do you mean?" I asked him.

"I know what I mean. So do you. The difference is that you haven't realized it yet."

His big face, puffed up like popcorn, split into a wide smile. It gave me confidence.

But I didn't have time to think about all that, because all of a sudden I saw the mop of Marie's hair go by. Her empty eyes were fixed on the noticeboard. Thank goodness she couldn't see it. People were crowding around it, laughing and joking. Just then the bell rang, and they all started drifting off towards their classes. I let myself be carried along by the crowd, doing my best not to be noticed. I watched Marie counting the steps to the staircase, concentrating hard. Meanwhile I was counting on my fingers. We just had to hold out for five more weeks. I realized she was confused by the scrum, which was jostling her around like a spinning top. I hurried over to her, hoping I wasn't lining myself up for a public slapping.

"Careful," I whispered, "the staircase is in the opposite direction!"

"Your voice sounds odd. What's going on?"

"Nothing. I've got a sore throat, so I've wrapped myself up in my jacket like an Egyptian mummy."

"Did you do the geometry?"

"Yes. I've got two copies. I'll keep the one with a mistake in it. Here you are."

"What's all this business about photos pinned on the noticeboard?" she asked as we were heading upstairs. "I can't work out what's going on. Everyone's laughing all around me and I'd like to share the joke!"

So then I really did say the first thing that came into my head.

"Oh, it's just some nonsense… Van Gogh took a picture of the biology teacher kissing the music teacher in the lab…"

"Hmm, that's odd, I wouldn't have thought they'd make a good couple."

Just then I got recognized in the corridor. But my enemies confined themselves to muttered comments, since they wanted to remain attached to their ears, and the others eyed me with respect, knowing the speed of my fists. Shame wasn't doing me any good at all just then. The maths teacher opened the door for us and gave me a wry look. She'd put some new thingies in her hair that made a big difference, even better than a facelift. I smiled vaguely at her.

At the end of the lesson I dawdled a bit, because I felt safest in the classroom. The teacher put away her things and since I still hadn't left she began to wipe the board.

"Anything wrong, Victor?"

"No, no, everything's just fine. Someone takes my picture and then I get dragged through the mud in front of hundreds of people. Otherwise everything's fine. But I'm told it does you good to feel ashamed once in a while…"

"I saw the photos. She's a very pretty girl. You should probably feel flattered, all things considered."

I frowned. Obviously, I wasn't going to go into all the details concerning Marie.

"She might be a pretty girl, but she's not my type. It was just a dirty trick my hormones played on me."

She smiled.

"By the way, since we're sharing confidences," I said, "I've noticed that these days your dead baby doesn't seem to weigh you down so much."

"That's right, Victor. He's gone back into my heart."

"That's good news."

After that neither of us dared say anything else, for fear of disrupting the delicate balance of our intimacy.

The day dragged on like a stretchy old snake. I avoided Marie because I was worried stiff that she'd want to know more about the photos. Between lessons, I saw Etienne waiting outside Lucky Luke's office, which was not a good sign. He told me he had big problems.

When he'd gone into class, the pupils were already there but not the teacher, so he'd had the bright idea of yelling out, "So then, any sex going on in here?" It was his bad luck that the teacher was in the little storeroom that opened onto the classroom. It was even worse luck that she was with the head teacher. Result: he'd been given a serious roasting.

"Then the head asked me what job I wanted to do later on," Etienne added. "So obviously I said I wanted to be a proctologist. She asked me what it involved, so I told her it meant taking care of anuses. So that's how I've ended up outside Lucky Luke's office."

"You're asking for trouble with that choice of profession."

"I really don't see what everyone's got against it as a specialism. It's no more disgusting than dentistry, maybe even less so. It's just the other end, that's all."

At last it was the end of the day. I'd tried so hard to avoid Marie, but now I was getting the feeling that it was she who was trying to avoid me. I could see Haisam settling into a game of chess with his father in the lodge, as if they were in a goldfish bowl. I waved and he gave me a firm little nod, as though to boost my morale. One day he was going to stop talking altogether, but it wouldn't matter because

241

some people don't need words to communicate. Just like others don't need eyes to see.

I started strolling home. Strangely, I no longer felt any hatred for Van Gogh. Haisam had explained that in the Nimzo-Indian Defence a full understanding of your situation is more powerful than your opponent's attack. Or something like that. I tried again to make sense of it all, but my brain worked too slowly.

Once my Honourable Egyptian had said, "I'm no more intelligent than you are, it's just that my brain works much faster."

It was a big difference, all the same. Imagine a champion cyclist winning the Tour de France and saying, "I'm not a better cyclist than you, I just pedal faster." These thoughts were going through my mind when my world fell apart. There she was, just in front of the church, in the square where we'd seen the boules players and where the fair had taken place. The look on her face was exactly the expression I imagined Jupiter would have worn when he was raging against his fellow gods. The only things missing were the thunderbolts and lightning. If it wasn't for the fact that I still had a shred of dignity, I'd have hurtled straight into the church like a torpedo. I'd have prayed in whatever way I could, on my knees, flat on my stomach or standing on my head. I'd have begged forgiveness from everyone, even Jupiter, because you never know.

Marie must have recognized my footsteps. She began to speak in a very low voice, even lower than usual, and that made it still worse – I'd have preferred her to shout at me.

"I know about the photos."

I tried to say something, but no sound came out. I must have looked like a fish without its fins.

"You could have told me," she said. "Because obviously, I can't see anything, as you know."

I was still unable to speak. I thought about the old films I used to watch on TV with Dad, in which the unmasked villain always copped a slap on the face.

"I felt a bit ridiculous when they told me who you were with in the photos. Not so much because of what the others would think – I don't really care about them – but still, it hurt my feelings."

"Feelings?" I asked, with a slight delay, as though we were in different time zones.

"Yes, feelings ... you know what I mean..."

"Yes, I know. 'Feelings: the ability to feel; to have an appreciative awareness. A complex emotional state involving susceptibility to impressions. See emotion,

243

passion.' I came across it yesterday in the dictionary."

Great idea to bring the dictionary into it! But sometimes it works, changing the subject... I felt like sharing with her my theory that defining things makes them less frightening... She stood stiffly in front of me, as though standing to attention... *For example, if you look up "cancer" in the dictionary you'll see that it comes from a Latin word meaning "crab" and that cuts it down to size a bit...* She was frowning... *Personally, I think that dictionaries were invented to make life feel less tragic. I wasn't surprised to learn that they were even written in Ancient Rome.*

Suddenly, she seemed to freeze and I thought, *Well, that's great, she's going to have a fit.* But instead her eyes started welling up with tears. It was strange because as they ran down her face I wasn't sure whether they made her eyes look more alive or even more dead. I found an almost clean tissue in my pocket and she blew her nose, which turned red. As red as my heart, which was wrung out like an old floor-cloth. I didn't dare make a move.

"Do you want to sit down?" I asked, feeling choked-up.

"Sit down?"

"Yes, on our bench."

Immediately she stiffened again. I saw the slap

244

coming. But it was too easy: I took a step to one side and of course she missed me. She spun around, lost her balance and fell to the ground. Her knees were skinned and bleeding a bit. This time there was absolutely no room for doubt: I was pathetic. Truly pathetic. I didn't even let her slap me, when it was the least I could have done. And she'd gone whirling through the air and collapsed into the dust, in front of the watching boules players. She struggled to get up, like a newborn foal that's unsteady on its feet. I held out a hand, forgetting she couldn't see it.

"Go away," she said quietly. "Go away, please. I don't want to see you any more."

I would feel terrible for days and days afterwards about that slap that didn't reach its target.

I ran home fast enough to beat the hundred metres record. My guilt had turned my heart to jelly. At home, Dad was writing a reply to some clients who'd put an advertisement in the Journal. A black fly had landed on the top of his head.

"You look rough. Has there been an earthquake? A tidal wave? Is it the plague? A hostile army at the gates of Paris?"

If only that was all it was. It would take too long to explain. And anyway, Marie had made me promise not to say anything, not even to the Honourable Egyptian, not even to Dad. I wasn't going to betray her again.

In the night it felt like there was a procession of tanks in my head, with nuclear submarines and battleships bringing up the rear.

The next day I got up and looked out into the yard. The Panhard had gone, leaving an empty space, a dry rectangle on the wet paving stones. When Dad's not here any more, I thought, that'll be an empty space too: another square hole with straight lines and no rough edges. I drank my hot chocolate and thought of Marie. She must be really mad at me; she'd probably never think of me in the same way again. The truth is, I'd lost a reason to feel proud, and life doesn't offer up many of those. What I'd liked, with Marie, was the feeling of being indispensible. Now I just felt like a piece of straw being swept along by the wind.

Before leaving for school, I turned my attention to wildlife conservation and the protection of birds in distress. It was actually a comfort, because I could see that my blackbird's wings were all shiny, as though they'd been varnished. I took him in the palm of my hand and his little feet scratched at me gently. At some point he would leave, which made me think that life is nothing but a stream of separations.

Heartsick, I limped through two more weeks. Spring had burst majestically into life like a flower, but the bud of my heart was withering, as if it had been scorched by a late frost. I stopped making an effort at school, because I wasn't doing it for anyone any more, so of course it was much less interesting. You need motivation to work, and my motivation was doing everything she could to avoid me. I watched her counting her steps at school: I was the only one to notice and I wondered why no one else did. I tried to go up to her a couple of times, but it was as though negative vibes enabled her to spot me approaching. What surprised me most was the casual, natural way she moved to a different desk. She really was extraordinarily gifted when it came to managing her life in darkness. Sometimes she brought her cello into class, because she had to have a music lesson straight after school. I heard her say that she'd asked her cello teacher to give her double lessons in the lead-up to the audition. I must say, I admired her deeply on the days she came in carrying that great big instrument.

During those two weeks of exile, I often

remembered the times I'd listened to her playing the cello and the strange feeling I'd had of being nothing and everything at the same time. You can say what you like, but there's nothing more wonderful than being the only one to share a secret with someone you admire.

Dad thought I looked peaky. I think he suspected my exiled state, but didn't like to ask about it, because it's not always easy for fathers and sons to open up to each other. Some nights I took my place next to him in the Panhard, on the meandering journey through small towns and suburbs, drifting together towards Paris until it swallowed us up. Every single time I wondered if we would ever get out of the city again. I remember driving up wide avenues, no one but us, as if the city was deserted after an air raid. Disused train tracks ... an old railway bridge... On the windscreen, I imagined I could see a reflection of the Paris map pinned up in Dad's office. I wondered how Dad had got to know all these bizarre people who wanted us to stay and listen to stories of their long-distant pasts. I always ended up falling asleep in the car and it felt like a miracle to wake up outside our ramshackle house. I'd go and see my blackbird, who was getting fatter, filling more and more of the shoebox, and scratching around in the yard with his beady little eyes darting everywhere. Maybe his troubles were over. At school, mine were very far from over. I had a go at trying to make Marie laugh, with a return to the wit that had once made me legendary. For example, one day someone asked what a stereotype was, so I said, "Someone who likes listening to loud music!"

But my heart wasn't in it and everyone had got out of the habit. No one laughed, least of all Marie.

One day, when I was wandering the corridors looking for the register for the maths teacher, I bumped into Lucky Luke. He came up to me, carrying a big book under his arm.

"Don't tell anyone... I'm going to hide in the gym to read for a while... If anyone's looking for me, you haven't seen me. I'll owe you one..."

"What's the book?"

"*Don Quixote*. I've finished *The Three Musketeers*, you see. I should think *Don Quixote* is roughly the same sort of thing. Have you read it?"

"I know there are windmills in it, but that's all."

"Windmills? Are you sure? I thought it was about battles and horses. And knights."

He looked disappointed.

"Anyway," I said, "it must be a very famous book, since even I've heard of it. How's the cycling going?"

"I came third last Sunday. Because I was completely worn out from reading too late the night before. It's crazy how tiring a big book is! Like climbing the Alps. Literature is hard work."

"Maybe I'll come and watch you race next Sunday... I'm quite bored at the moment. I need something to do. Perhaps I could sell chips to the spectators..."

"What's the matter with you?"

"I don't want to offend you, but you wouldn't understand..."

"Are you sure about that?"

"Quite sure. You don't know the facts."

"Is it something to do with those photos the other day?"

"Not exactly the photos themselves, but the consequences. Van Gogh really got one over on me, with that stunt. Checkmate. Ah well, I'll see what can be done with a Nimzo-Indian Defence."

I waited to see what effect my words would have. Lucky Luke seemed to be mulling them over.

"The what defence? Is that karate?"

"No, of course not. It's a chess term. A Nimzo-Indian Defence consists in showing your opponent that your understanding of the situation is greater than the dangers presented by the situation."

I hoped he wouldn't ask any more questions, because then I'd have been stuck. I'd told him everything I knew about the subject, and I still didn't get exactly what it meant. But now and then the mist cleared a bit: I was beginning to think that perhaps one day I would understand and that I should trust my Honourable Egyptian.

"Well, anyway, I'll leave you to get on with your Chinese Defence," said Lucky Luke.

"Indian, sir, Indian…"

"Whatever."

At the end of that day, I went to see Haisam in the lodge. He'd missed all the afternoon's lessons because he and his father had to finish the Moscow 1963 tournament. No one minded, because in any event he already knew everything there was to know. I arrived in the middle of the third game.

"Good timing," said the Honourable Egyptian, without looking up. "Look at this: Botvinnik proposes exchanging queens on the thirteenth move. A work of art or what?"

"Magnificent," I said, to avoid upsetting him.

I watched them play for a while. Now and

then Haisam would pass me the bowl of sweets. Afterwards I went home to Dad, my spirits sagging softly, just like Turkish delight.

10

When I arrived at school the next day, the playground looked completely different. The community police were there, some setting out red and white cones to create lanes, others installing and testing mini traffic lights. At the back, a guy was unloading go-karts and bikes from a lorry marked ROAD SAFETY EDUCATION, and lining them up. I looked for Marie in the crowd of kids, but I couldn't see her. And of course I realized straight away the danger she was in. She was going to get lost in the complicated labyrinth the police were laying out in the playground: Road Safety would be her undoing. But I'd seen the danger and could do something about it, so there was a chance it could be averted. Hope flickered at the heart of my anguish. *Thank you, Haisam,*

I thought. *Thank you for the Nimzo thingy!* Then the bell rang and we had to get in line.

The first lesson was history. Luckily, I was sitting near the window. A breath of spring air stroked my face. While the others were delving into the depths of the past, I could keep an eye on the playground. The minutes ticked by and still there was no sign of Marie. I didn't know whether to be worried or relieved. I pictured her barrelling into the middle of the go-karts, bikes and road signs as if she was entering a hostile little town. She wouldn't have a clue where she was. She would be utterly humiliated – disgraced even – and it would be the end of all our hopes.

I completely lost track of what was going on in the lesson. I think it was about some period when kings and princes spent half their time trying to assassinate each other, the other half trying to escape, and a further half trying to have sons or win wars. A total fiasco in fact, which didn't make me feel very hopeful for the future of the human race. But these were my own views and wouldn't have interested the teacher: he was a very serious man who wore a hearing aid, which made him look as though he was in constant communication with the ancient kings of France. I called him Beethoven, on account of the ear trouble.

Then I heard the school gate squeak. I was sure it was Marie, arriving late again. It must be taking her longer to get to school, counting all her steps in the way she'd explained to me. Maybe she even got lost sometimes, without me there to be Ariadne's thread. I imagined her alone in the empty streets, trying to find her way by groping around everywhere. Thinking about that made my heart shrivel like a withered apple, all wrinkled and empty.

I watched her as she came into the playground, walking mechanically like an automaton. But her steps were hesitant: she must have sensed that everything was in disarray. One, two, three, right... one, two, left. She bumped into a cone, stood motionless for a few seconds like a robot recalculating its route, and set off again purposefully in the opposite direction – only to stumble straight into a go-kart. At the back of the playground a policeman was watching her suspiciously. I don't want to sound smug, but I'd seen the catastrophe coming. Mind you, catastrophes aren't that hard to predict, you can usually bank on there being at least one in the offing. Experience has taught me that, too.

Marie was hopelessly lost between a fake red light and a fake one-way sign. Everything around her was fake. She was going round in circles: she must have been calculating and recalculating, but she wasn't getting anywhere. She was like a pinball bouncing off one thing after another. The worst of it was that the other kids in the class, and presumably in all the classes that looked out over the playground, were beginning to enjoy the spectacle, like ancient Romans at the arena, waiting for a bloodbath. They were nudging each other, sharing their amusement. We were done for: it was glaringly obvious that she couldn't see anything. And then, as if I was spring-loaded, I jumped to my feet and before I had time to think I was standing stiffly in front of the teacher.

"I've got to go, I've got diarrhoea," I said.

"Diarrhoea?"

"Yes. A bad case of the runs. Never happened to you?"

My words took a little time to filter through to his brain, partly because of the hearing aid and partly because of the surprise. And then it looked as though a head of steam was building up behind his eyes, obscuring his vision.

"You asked for details, so I gave you details!" I said.

Perhaps he was waiting for instructions from the ancient kings of France to come through his earpiece. So in the end I just left.

I headed towards Marie in the playground. There were faces pressed up against all the windows, watching us. It was complete pandemonium in the classrooms and the teachers were in a state about the lack of respect for their authority. As I walked into the arena, I could almost hear the public baying for our death. Sometimes it's useful to have historical references at your fingertips.

I followed the lanes laid out by the road safety guys and caught up with Marie at the end of a cul-de-sac. She must have heard me, because she said, "Is that you, Victor?"

"Yes, it's me, it's Ariadne's thread. Your very own path finder."

She looked relieved. Maybe it wasn't all over between us.

"Are you still mad at me?" I asked, though it was a strange moment to choose.

She blushed scarlet, but I couldn't tell if it was out of anger or love. Or both.

"Yes, I'm mad at you. But at the same time I know I'll never love anyone like you. Though if I could see clearly, I'd give you a good slap and that would make me feel a whole lot better."

"Hang on, I'll get a bit closer."

I didn't want her to miss me like last time. I stood right in front of her.

"Go ahead."

Of course, as soon as her slap struck home, everyone at the windows burst into applause, whistling and cheering, with the furious teachers in the background trying to calm things down. The policeman, who was still stationed towards the back of the playground, must have wondered what on earth he'd got into. I was seeing stars in every colour of the rainbow and my ears were buzzing as if they were full of hornets. She hadn't held back. I'd never known that being hurt so bad could feel so good.

Peace had returned after the great storm.

"OK, now follow me. Can you hear my footsteps?"

"I'm following you."

"Are you holding the thread tight?"

"Yes. And I'm not going to let it go again."

And that's how we crossed the playground, watched by all the kids who were now leaning out of the windows, a weird mixture of disappointment, mockery and admiration on their faces. I don't know what more entertainment they were expecting. The bell rang for break. We were definitely going to be in hot water with the school authorities. I thought of Lucky Luke.

"Quickly," I said to Marie, "give me the name of a really well-known book that I can get out of the school library."

"Why? You want to go and read during break? Can't we spend a bit of time together?"

"No, I'll explain later. It's very important – otherwise we're going to have a problem. We'll be singled out, separated and slung into exile."

"Exile? What exile?"

"Oh, never mind, it's a theory of Dad's about love and stuff... So, come on, the book? For someone who's come to literature late and wants to catch up. Just stop trying to understand for once!"

"All right... I'll trust you. Let's see... What's he interested in?"

"Cycling mostly."

"In that case there's a book by Antoine Blondin about the Tour de France. If he likes cycling, nothing could be better."

I absolutely had to get hold of this book before I was summoned to explain my behaviour – they were sure to describe it as "unspeakable" and "scandalous". We'd caused uproar in the school and wasted police time, which just goes to show it doesn't take many people to make a big impact. It was a good enough reason to be suspended. The library had the book in stock. I immediately registered for loans, and it was odd to see my name on the list. I flicked through the book as I was leaving: it was just the ticket. You could see the cyclists fly off the page, hear the roars of the spectators, smell the performance-enhancing substances... Yet at the same time there was something sad about it, which touched your heart. That's the magic of literature.

Then I heard them calling Marie and me over the loudspeaker. We met up with Lucky Luke in the corridor outside his office. He looked unshaven and seemed irritated by us. He said that he had to take us to see the head, that it didn't give him any pleasure but that we'd made a spectacle of ourselves and disrupted all the morning's lessons.

"Wait here for me," he said. "I'll be back in two minutes. I've just got some papers to tidy up."

He disappeared into his mysterious office – he hardly ever came out of there these days. So I took a big gamble and followed him, leaving Marie on her own. He started when he saw me come in. He was sitting in a very big armchair, looking very small. Behind the desk I spotted a new bookshelf with two books neatly arranged in alphabetical order: Cervantes just before Dumas. Blondin would fit very nicely in front of them.

"What are you doing here, Victor?"

"I wanted to talk to you about something and since we're about to be bawled at by the head, well, I think it's going to be hard for me to broach the subject if I don't do it now."

There were posters on the walls of champion cyclists busting a gut to complete a sprint or a mountain stage, sweating like chickens on a spit.

I wasn't sure how to start, but I didn't have much time so in the end I just plunged in.

"So. Did you like *Don Quixote?*"

He waved his hand dismissively.

"Not much. I was disappointed."

"Why?"

"It's not – how can I put it? – it's not a *serious* book. I don't like it when characters are made fun of. Because, at the end of the day, Don Quixote is nothing but a barmy old fool. I can't be doing with that sort of thing. Have you got any other suggestions?"

Ceremoniously, I held out the book. He snatched it from me and began to sniff at it, as though he might gobble it up.

"I hope there's a bit of tragedy in it at least."

"No idea. You'll have to wait and see."

The telephone rang and Lucky Luke answered. It was the head.

"Right, we have to go. Still, you haven't got much to complain about. When I was at boarding school, if you did something wrong, you had to get down on your knees in the head teacher's empty office. You had to wait like that for fifteen minutes ... half an hour ... and then a bell would ring, the head would barge in and give you a whack, or several whacks depending on the crime, without ever saying a word. Then you had to stay on your knees until another bell rang to let you know you could clear off."

"Things were harder in those days."

"Once I escaped by stealing the porter's bicycle. I did three hundred and fifty kilometres in three days and since then I've never been able to get enough of it..."

"You had a pretty weird childhood!"

He seemed flattered by the note of admiration in my voice.

"Do you remember yesterday when we bumped into each other in the corridor and you were on your way to hide in the gym to read *Don Quixote?* Huh? Well, you said you'd owe me one."

"OK. I'll see what I can do. But I don't know what you were thinking of, putting on such a display! It's not nice to make fun of the blind. Coming from you, it doesn't surprise me all that much, though I'm shocked that your girlfriend would do such a thing."

"It was a stupid bet. But it was my idea and I think it would be best just to punish me. Because I'm sure that if you punish her too, her parents will send her away to boarding school and you'll lose your best student."

"Are her parents really that strict?"

"Yes, sure they are, I know them well. The father's an auction ear, she'll never hear the end of it! As soon as they find out, I guarantee you they'll start packing, and that'll be the last you'll see of your star pupil."

Then Marie and I followed Lucky Luke down the corridor.

"Right, let me go in first," he said, outside the head's office.

Suddenly, I had a brainwave.

"I know, tell her I've got a brilliant idea for a way to make amends."

"What kind of idea?" said Lucky Luke.

"Well, I was thinking we could put on a cello concert for the school ... something really distinguished, for connoisseurs."

"But you don't play the cello."

"No, but I can turn the pages for the cellist."

Lucky Luke disappeared inside the head's office.

"Have you gone crazy?" asked Marie. "A cello concert? What's got into you?"

"No, don't you see. It's a really good idea. You don't get it: with all that palaver earlier it's not going to take long for people to realize that you're as blind as a bat. I'm pretty sure some people suspect already. Do you think Van Gogh is going to miss such a golden opportunity to bring us down? A concert will shut everyone up, especially if it looks like you're reading the score."

"Actually that's not such a bad plan... Maybe you're right... The important thing is to gain time. We've only got to hold out for three more weeks."

Her eyes were shining like little candles. I noticed that her shirt was buttoned wrongly: details like that could catch us out too.

She sighed.

"There's another problem."

"What?"

"The road safety drill. I'll have to drive – bike or go-kart. Either way it's a disaster."

At this point I was clean out of ideas. If she made an excuse to go and see the nurse, there was a risk she might be examined and get found out. I was still an amateur, compared with Haisam, who was always at least fifteen moves ahead of his opponent. I thought it best to say nothing. You can often be credited with intelligence if you keep your mouth shut and look mysterious.

The outcome of our visit to the head was that I would be made to sweep one of the corridors and Marie would give a free concert for the whole school, including parents. Ah well, horses for courses!

At the end of the morning I wound up at Haisam's, completely bushed. I didn't even have the strength to go to the canteen. Moral anxieties are far more exhausting than physical exertion, I find. I felt totally drained. Haisam was sitting on a tiny chair with his elbows on the table, looking at the chessboard as though he was trying to hypnotize it and get it to cough up all its secrets. His enormous stomach, packaged in his inevitable checked shirt, was touching the edge of the table.

"What are you doing?" I asked.

"Nothing."

"What do you mean, nothing?"

"Just nothing. It's the start of the Sabbath. We're not supposed to do anything, so I'm not doing anything."

"One day, you really will have to explain to me why half-Egyptian Turks observe the Sabbath. And anyway I thought it didn't start until the evening?"

"I can start it whenever I like. For me, midday on Friday is when it starts, because as a chess player I'm always one move ahead. There's nothing to explain. And it doesn't bother anyone. Does it bother you, for example?"

"I really couldn't care less. Anyway, I barely know where Turkey is: on the map I got it muddled up with India."

"Well, Europe and the Arabs should have left us alone in the nineteenth century... They had us for breakfast, so now in revenge we observe the Sabbath. To annoy Europe and the Arabs, if you like. From midday on Friday, if that's the way we want it."

I couldn't really make head nor tail of what he was talking about. Watching the way he was staring at his chessboard, I wondered if he was feeling quite all right. His lips moved now and then, so I knew he was playing an imaginary game. I took a deep breath.

"Haisam," I said, "I've got problems."

He didn't look up.

"I know."

"I know you know. You never say anything, but you know everything before anyone else. Like the crocodiles in the Nile."

"Always a few moves ahead, like in chess. So, she's blind then?"

He nodded to himself. He was really becoming enormous. My dear Egyptian gradually seemed to be turning into a mythological being.

"Nobody must know it, or we're done for. But the thing is, with this afternoon's road safety drill it's not looking good."

Haisam moved one of his pieces and laid down his imaginary opponent's king. He sighed and took a piece of Turkish delight.

"And yet," he said, "from what I saw this morning you seem to have grasped the basic principles of the Nimzo-Indian Defence. But now you're stuck. Look..."

He pointed at the chessboard as though the solution could be found there.

"So what now?" I was beginning to panic.

"So Nimzovich wasn't just defending. He was also attacking, *by controlling the centre from a distance and blockading his opponent.* That's all there is to it. Nothing could be clearer."

Haisam's father appeared at that moment and turned on a tiny radio. The news wasn't exactly cheerful: bombs all over the place, in cafés and cinemas. And schools. The whole world was calling for vengeance, even those who'd planted the bombs. It was kicking off just about everywhere and I felt a bit of a schmuck with my worries. *Controlling the centre ... blockading...* I stood up.

"Going already?" asked the noble and honourable Egyptian. "Have you got it?"

"I think so."

He raised his great paw in farewell.

"You're a prince, my man," he said solemnly.

Well, that brought tears to my eyes. But then I'd been feeling ultra sensitive for some time. I was like a sponge, you only had to press lightly for tears to appear.

There wasn't much time left. I had to find Marcel urgently. Only he could tell me how to get in touch with Etienne, who'd been suspended again. I had to talk to him. I criss-crossed the playground, zigzagging back and forth in all directions, and finally located him playing in goal in a football match.

"I've got to speak to Etienne!"

I must have looked like a raving lunatic.

"You look weird, like you're going off your head. Is it all that hoo-ha earlier that's got you into this state?"

"How can I find Etienne!"

"It's easy enough. He gets so bored at home that he hangs around outside the school gates every day. Anyway, he's been behaving really oddly recently and he looks ill. You need to keep an eye on him. Now go away – I don't want to let a goal through because of you."

Just then I saw Van Gogh charging headlong towards me with the ball. It was obvious he was deliberately missing the goal in order to knock me off my feet, so I dodged to the right. The ball ended up on a roof, the match had to stop and the other players ripped into him. I made time to give him the finger, discreetly. An intimate, almost friendly gesture, just between the two of us.

I took up a look-out position by the gates like a monkey waiting for peanuts. I missed lunch. I was hungry and it took a lot of self-denial, which was a word I'd heard the head use when I was in her office. I hadn't exactly understood it, but it seemed appropriate to my situation all the same. It feels good to enrich your vocabulary: even if you only get it approximately right, it's like a breath of fresh air. And so I waited, one eye on the playground clock and the other on the road Etienne would come down.

I'd almost lost hope when I saw his silhouette in the distance. I started waving wildly, as though I'd been washed up on a desert island. As soon as he got close I pounced.

"Etienne! Etienne! I need you!"

"You need me?"

It was true, he did have a strange, preoccupied look about him.

"Yes, I need you. Listen, there's not much time. I'll pay you back whenever you want and however you want. Here's the thing: in fifteen minutes it's the road safety drill and we've all got to schlep around a course on bikes or in go-karts. I really, really need it not to happen."

"So? What am I supposed to do about it?"

He was playing hard to get. I felt the blood rising to my head.

"You're going to go to the nearest telephone box. You're going to call the school and explain that a bomb's been planted. You'll need to disguise your voice. Bombs are being planted everywhere these days, it's become a kind of sport. So why not in our school? Planes have even been cancelled because of bomb threats. So they'll almost certainly evacuate us all. In chess it's called 'controlling the centre from a distance' and 'blockading your opponent'. Then you have to get right away from here – either go home or go somewhere people will see you."

He was listening with a frown on his face. You could tell the wheels were slowly going round.

"Can't I stay and take photos?"

"No, of course not, use your head… When you're a proctologist, if you don't think things through better than this you'll be in a fine mess!"

"OK, I don't mind doing you a favour. And anyway it's quite a fun idea. But on one condition…"

"What?" I asked, keeping one eye on the policemen in charge of the vehicles. "Quick, there's not much time."

"Well, you see that girl over there with the pink bow in her hair?"

I hesitated, but took a gamble.

"Warty Toadskin?"

"Yes. But don't call her that, it upsets me. Look, I want you to write her a love song, from me. Something that will highlight her qualities. Her moral *and* her physical qualities, please. Something distinguished."

I stopped myself from laughing, partly because he looked so serious and partly because I didn't want to waste any more time.

"All right. I'll give it to you the day after tomorrow."

"How about tomorrow?"

"No, the day after tomorrow, because you can't just call up poetic passion to order."

Etienne ran off towards the telephone box.

The head was first to come out of her office, looking alarmed, followed by the school assistants. The fire alarm began to wail. Lucky Luke took a while to appear. He looked vacant, as though the situation had nothing to do with him. A continuous stream of pupils began to pour out of every door. Since Lucky Luke was still doing nothing about it, the head began to shout at him.

"What on earth are you waiting for? Can't you see the chaos out here? Any chance you could shift yourself? You're supposed to be the man in charge!"

The Man in Charge gazed blankly over the playground as though he was looking through a thick pane of glass. Then he got us to line up, in a very half-hearted and offhand way: he was obviously miles away.

"Why are you in such a terrible state?" I asked him. "Have you got some personal problems?"

"It's the book on the Tour de France by Antoine Blondin. You should never have given me something so explosive."

"But it's a good book," I said, taking a guess.

"It's not about how good it is... I think literature is sending me round the bend... I was hiding behind the ping-pong tables and then I just ran onto the basketball court and ... do you know what I shouted out, all on my own, in the gym?"

"No."

"I was on page thirteen and I yelled out at the top of my voice, 'Anquetil, I love you!'. Jacques Anquetil was the first person to win the Tour de France five times, you know. I hope no one heard me. All of a sudden I understood where poor old Don Quixote was coming from."

I was impressed. Don Quixote on wheels – it was quite an appealing idea.

He shook himself.

"Literature completely takes it out of you, there's no question about it."

He scratched his bristly square head.

Then the rumour started going round that the phone call had been made by a certain Darth Vader and there'd been a lot of very heavy breathing in between the threats. I checked, because I wouldn't have put it past him, that Etienne wasn't anywhere around watching us in his big black cape and decidely alarming mask connected to an oxygen cylinder.

I waited for Marie, and we joined the stream of people making their way out through the school's main entrance.

"Do you think it was a miracle?" she asked.

"Must have been," I replied.

"Yes, it must have been, a real miracle."

She winked at me and I was bowled over.

11

We glided unstoppably towards summer. Leaves spread over the trees and huge spots spread over the boys' faces. I got a new one every day: I tried to count them, but I gave up at seventy-two. It was like the surface of the moon. Dad had bought me a sort of whitish lotion and applied it to my face every evening. At first, it itched and after ten minutes my face was on fire. But he insisted that it had to be left on for at least half an hour, so to distract me he'd sit me down in front of some historical TV documentary. Historical events made him very anxious and I think he saw my acne as a kind of revolution that needed to be quelled. Afterwards I was allowed to go and clean up. I looked as though I'd given myself a tan with a blowtorch, but Dad thought it improved my appearance.

"You're as handsome as a prince," he'd say. "Now go and shave!"

It was like scrubbing my face with sandpaper. The only good thing about this time of raging hormones was that we were all in the same boat. Hormones are very democratic that way. Nobody dared to tease me about it at school. We didn't even give Warty Toadskin a hard time, because we were all getting to look more and more like her. And anyway it hadn't stopped her getting a boyfriend. Only Etienne and Marie were aware that I'd had a hand in bringing the two lovebirds together. It was the first time I'd kept something from my noble Egyptian and it made me feel good, this sign of independence.

As far as Warty's interior beauty had been concerned, that was easy, I'd just used my imagination. But her physical beauty had posed more of a challenge.

I showed Dad the poem, just so he could check the spelling, because overall I thought it sounded quite tasteful:

Well I know how they call you Wharty Toadskin,

How they also say you're shaped like a muffin,

And yet me, I adore your humongous nose!

Real beauty's within: my love is like a red, red nose!

Thighs as vigorous as yours I grately admire,

You flex their mussels at netball and my heart's on fire.

Then you rise off the ground despite your great size:

Oh! Round as the ball, but like a rocket in my eyes!

And later in the canteen, I watch your jaws chew,

Divine creature, as you wolf down potatoe's and stew.

So I gaze upon you gobbling, my heart full of love,

Kissing your dark moustashe is all I dream of.

I hope, once you've gorged, you'll say you'll be mine:

Now look kindly upon me and I'll really feel fine!

Dad went pale and then the top of his head flushed red. It was obvious he was impressed and overcome with paternal pride.

"Did you notice," I said, "that the first letters of

each line make a word? It's striking, don't you think?"

"Warty doesn't have an h."

He sank back into the armchair and looked at me thoughtfully, rubbing his chin.

"I wrote it on my own," I added, a bit self-consciously.

"I should hope so," said Dad. "Two of you would have been overkill."

"Except for 'my love is like a red, red rose', which I found in a book at school."

"Get some paper. We're going to improve it."

"Don't you like it? I think it's sensational!"

"Yes, I like it, but we're still going to improve it. Just a few little things here and there. Don't you think Mick Jagger ever tries to improve his lyrics? And that poet – Ronsard – do you think he'd still be reducing us to tears if he hadn't made an effort to lick his poems into shape?"

In the end I gave Etienne the version Dad and I had reworked, but to be honest I wasn't all that happy about it. The spelling, that's one thing, but in terms of the overall flavour, I preferred the original version. Marie said I was like Christian in the play *Cyrano de Bergerac*. It didn't mean much to me, but apparently it's about a man who writes a letter to a girl on behalf of another man. Still, one should never complain about being compared to a hero of literature.

"Do you think he needed to check his grammar, this Christian?" I asked her.

Anyway, here's what the final version looked like:

Since I first heard your name,
I've felt completely lame.
Love's arrow's in my heart:
It's tearing me apart.
When I see your little hand
Taking notes in class, it's grand.
When I see your fingers scribble,
I'd love to take a nibble.
If I could only be your pen
I'd surely never be sad again.
My ink would be my tears
Because in all my years
I've never been so close
To such a lovely nose.
Your chubby cheeks, your granite jaw
You've no idea how I adore!
I know I can be a bit of a clown.
I know that you might turn me down:
But I can only do my best
To make my heart a little nest
Where the love of my life can rest.

It was funny to see Etienne and Warty Toadskin, arm in arm, holding hands, gazing into each other's eyes. I'd achieved something at least. To start with, I'd assumed Etienne was only attracted to Warty Toadskin on account of the hormones, because he had a theory.

"You see," he'd explained, "it's the ugliest girls who are the most up for it."

"Oh, right…"

"Of course, it's logical. Warty Toadskin is the ugliest girl in school, isn't she?"

"Well, one of the ugliest anyway. You'd need specialists to choose between them."

"So Warty Toadskin must be one of the most up for it in the school, if not the most."

It was one way of looking at things. Marie had explained to me that it was a syllogism, which was apparently something to watch out for because it could lead you to the wrong conclusion. She gave some example involving Socrates, but I can't remember how it went. Anyway, since I wasn't exactly sure what Etienne meant by being up for it, part of the reasoning escaped me. But then as time went on, it became obvious that Etienne's theory didn't hold together, because he'd properly fallen in love. I like to see a theory come crashing down: it's a sign of the real world breaking free and slipping out through the cracks. He'd even settled down and become much calmer: love never leaves you unscathed. One day he came to find me, looking bothered.

"You see things in a poetic sort of way," he said. "Do you know what would be a good gift to give to a girl? Something subtle."

"I don't know, maybe flowers."

"Flowers? No chance, she gets hay fever."

"Then some perfume. Yes, that would be good, perfume. That's what people usually give, flowers or perfume. Or a book, but that's really for intellectuals and for when it gets serious."

He seemed really anxious.

"Or you could invite her out for a meal," I went on. "Candlelight is romantic and good for revitalizing a relationship. I once saw a film on TV about stuff like that. By the way, have you told her about your future profession?"

"What do you mean?"

"Have you told her you want to be a proctologist?"

He explained that since he'd fallen in love he'd lost interest in bum holes.

"So, for the gift, then, what do you think you'll choose?"

"I'm going to invite her to the cinema to see a horror film and I'll buy her some popcorn. I think that would be the most sophisticated thing to do."

I don't know why, but on the spur of the moment, I asked him, "I know I'm changing the subject, but do you know if our old cabin is still standing?"

"Why? Do you want to go back there to rehearse the band?"

"No, I just wanted to know if it was still in good shape."

"Yes, it's still standing, still got its bunks and everything, nice and comfortable... Hey, maybe that's where I should invite her..."

Etienne wasn't the only one to have been changed by love's magic. One day I noticed that our maths teacher wasn't limping any more. She was walking perfectly normally, even confidently. The weight of her baby must have left her for good and her life surely felt lighter again. Sometimes in lessons she had a dreamy look on her face and a vague smile. She was clearly finding it difficult to concentrate and would rather have been talking to us about something other than cosines, tangents and proportions. In the glorious month of June, it's impossible to work up any interest in maths. I was sure she'd met someone with whom she could ... well, you know ... and that's far more interesting than all those stacks of numbers, even for specialists. These days she wore skirts, which showed a sort of flirtatious friskiness, and glittery earrings that hypnotized me during lessons. In fact I even began to think quite highly of her. Not to the same extent as Marie, Haisam or Dad, but quite highly all the same.

I was sure now that Marie and I would make it to the audition. Since the concert, everything had become much easier, because there was no longer any reason for suspicion. Everyone had thought that Marie was following the score closely, although actually she knew the music by heart. We'd agreed on a sign so that I would know the right moment to turn the page. I'd had to practise, because it's not all that easy to turn pages in the correct way. Even in life it can be really hard to turn the page. Dad had explained that turning the page was a figure of speech for learning to forget and put to one side any painful parts of one's life. I could see that this was a sort of invitation.

"And about our old life with Mum, did you manage to turn the page, Dad?"

But he wasn't a great one for sharing confidences

and he often took refuge behind the huge old Panhard. He wanted to put me off the scent by talking about the manufacture of Panhard PL17s in Uruguay, reeling off a ridiculous list of chassis numbers.

"The *page*, Dad, did you manage to turn it?"

He took a deep breath.

"Yes, but it wasn't a comic book, I can tell you!"

I could see he wasn't sure I'd get what he meant, but I nodded gravely to show that I was used to parables and understood his feelings.

"But still we're happy, Dad, the two of us, aren't we?"

"Of course we're happy!" he said, slapping me on the back to encourage me.

Marie had told me that I was very skilled in the specialist art of page-turning and that when she was famous she would take me on as page-turner, an essential role if concerts are to run smoothly. She explained that there were some great musicians, hugely talented, who'd never given their best because they didn't have a good page-turner.

"I'm very lucky to have found mine straight away," she said.

To be honest, I couldn't quite see why she needed a page-turner, given her visual circumstances, but

I wasn't going to argue with her about it. And anyway, people you love often tend to make you feel indispensible, even when you know perfectly well that you're of no use whatsoever.

On the evening of the concert the audience were rooted to their seats, all hunched up and almost embarrassed to breathe. I'd put Haisam and his father in the front row.

"It's the Sabbath," said the Honourable Egyptian, "but I'm making an exception for once. Not so much for the music but for the pleasure of seeing a whole crowd of people conned by a blind girl and a dummy."

Normally I'd have been put out, but with Haisam you always had to look beyond the obvious, so I could see that he was actually paying me a great compliment.

On the stage I felt completely exposed: I don't think I'd have felt much different if I'd been stripped naked. Every time I turned a page it felt like taking off another item of clothing but then, with invisible stitches, Marie's bow seemed to knit me something new to wear. When it was over I realized I was sweating and my heart was racing. The school VIPs and the local big cheeses came up to congratulate Marie – and me too a bit, just to be polite. Marie looked straight into their eyes: how on earth did she know how to find them?

We thought we'd got over the final hurdle. Two weeks to go. Like Moses parting the Red Sea, all we had to do was lift a finger and any dangers fell away. At school, I no longer knew whether I was protecting her or she was protecting me. Although she was defenceless and I was her shield, her vulnerability had given me something too: for the first time I felt that there was a real purpose to me being at school. For example, if she was asked to read a text it was I who spoke up, but everybody seemed to find it normal, as though we'd fused into one. A bit like Laurel and Hardy. I must say I liked that, to start with. And then, as we got closer and closer to the audition, I felt something I could never have imagined: I began to dread the end of the school year. I didn't just feel slightly apprehensive, I felt a real anxiety that gripped my throat during the day and made my heart quake at night. This was going to be an immense page that I'd never be able to turn. One day, as we walked towards the music academy, I spoke to Marie about it.

"You see," I said, "it's not a great situation. School

has always been a disaster for me. Even at nursery school, Dad said I had some trouble fitting in. Then I had to repeat the last year of primary school. And then this year everything changed in one fell swoop. It's the first time anyone's *really* depended on me. And that's not nothing. I really believe that to be happy in life, you just need to feel useful. You see, it'll soon be the holidays... You'll be off to your school for musical geniuses and so on... And me..."

"And you?"

She was looking at me, smiling mischievously, as though I was talking nonsense.

"Well, it'll be exile all over again... I'll be on my own. Everything will go back to how it was before. Except that it's not fun any more, spending my time hiding the toilet paper. They're all free to take a dump whenever they want, I've got other things to think about now. I've risen above all that. Sometimes, I swear, I find myself hoping that you'll fail your audition so that you can stay here with me. But of course it's not in your nature to fail things, just like it's not in mine to succeed exactly. My life is like Dad's, following strange paths that aren't quite straight. And next year, well, I'll be the one who's blind."

I could see she was trying to understand, which

was very kind and thoughtful of her. So then, I don't know what got into me: instead of stopping right there and keeping my dignity, I chose to ramp up the emotional content. Lowering my eyes and speaking in a solemn voice, as though I was making an important statement, I said, "My life in truth only began the day I met you."

"So you've heard of that?"

"Heard of what?"

"Well, that quote from Louis Aragon, 'My life in truth begins…'"

"Oh? That's by him? What's he called, did you say?"

"Louis Aragon. A great poet. Sometimes a little sentimental and overblown, but still…"

"That's funny, I could have sworn he was an aviator. It just goes to show it's not difficult to come up with fancy phrases. You just have to let yourself go a bit…"

We walked on for a few minutes in silence. The trees and houses all around seemed to be in sharp focus, as sometimes happens at the beginning of summer. I thought about how I could put my feelings across.

"The thing is," I sighed at last, "next year, my heart will be written in Braille."

I was quite pleased with the way I'd put it, because it perfectly expressed everything that was in my heart and everything that I feared in the future. Marie stopped in front of me and squeezed her little eyes tightly as though she was praying for them to see one last time. And then, something amazing happened. She slipped her arms around me until she could clasp them behind my back, and gently, very gently, she pressed her face to my chest, bending her knees a little because she was taller than me. "No one will ever say anything so beautiful to me," she said after a few minutes. "For as long as you say things like that to me, I'm sure I'll be able to play music that will make the stars tremble in the sky."

"Do you think so?" I replied, like an idiot.

"Yes."

And then we burst out laughing, because we were still at an age when laughter and tears are easily confused. Later on our hearts teach us to understand the difference.

Dad often asked me now to go to El Dorado with him and help with his deliveries. I was really pleased. He'd probably decided that I'd done well over the course of the year and that I'd earned the right to be given some responsibilities. What I remember most, as we set off into the night, is the headlamps from cars coming towards us from time to time, making me blink. At the warehouse, I would load up the car, checking items off on Dad's list. Then I'd go and join him in his "office". We never planned our route, so we'd still travel in complicated circles around Paris, as if it was a labyrinth. Sometimes Dad would share his reflections on life in general, on history and on the way the world was going – or as he saw it, going to the dogs.

"Know something, Victor?"

"What, Dad?"

"The truth is that ever since Citroën liquidated the Panhard business, well, everything's gone belly-up."

"Such a dirty trick for Citroën to play."

"Once upon a time no one would have dared to liquidate the first French car manufacturer like that. Nowadays you only come across Panhards in South America and Cuba. Or Vietnam."

"It's a shame, Dad, but that's life."

"Life sucks, if you want my opinion."

So there we were, father and son, travelling through the summer nights and calling on all Dad's clients in turn. There were so many of them that their faces and addresses eventually got all jumbled up in my head. One who I remember a little more clearly than most was an old gentleman who wanted Dad to supply him with anything to do with Charles de Gaulle. He always offered us a cup of tea and before we left he would look me straight in the eye and say, "Never forget: your father's the best. If he'd wanted, he could have worked in … in … in America, that's it. The best, you see, be sure and remember that."

"Yes, the best. I'll remember … or at least I'll try. The best."

Once I asked Dad about it.

"Why is that old client of yours always telling me you're the best? The best at what?"

"I don't know."

"And why America?"

"I don't know."

"It's a bit odd though, don't you think?"

"I think he must be confusing me with someone else. Collectors are often deranged. And anyway, being the best doesn't mean much. Paul and Jean Panhard were also the best, but it didn't stop Citroën doing the dirty on them."

"As far as I'm concerned, Dad, he's right and you are the best. Really and truly the best."

He drove on, looking straight ahead as though he hadn't heard me. I let a few seconds go by while I watched him out of the corner of my eye.

"I don't know quite what it is you're the best at," I went on. "I don't even know what it means, but I'm still sure you're the best."

It was weird travelling through the empty city, submerged in darkness. We'd go back over our tracks several times, as though we were lost yet again, and I'd often end up wondering whether Dad's driving was actually completely random, despite his self-assured and confident air.

The red lights seemed to take ages to change and I had the impression that Dad was driving more and more slowly. Perhaps we'd go round and round in circles until the end of time in that massive Panhard, our only frail link with reality. Gradually, I'd fall asleep and Dad would deal with the last few clients on his own. Sometimes, I'd wake up briefly and think of Marie, who really was the best. I tried to hope that one day it would do her some good.

We'd been so lucky and got away with so much that I'd begun to believe that we'd get to the audition without getting caught out. But it's a mistake to be too optimistic, as I'd learnt from watching historical documentaries with Dad. Still, it all seemed so easy that it was even beginning to be fun. And Marie was getting prettier and prettier, with all her red curls sparkling as they tumbled onto her shoulders. So that filled me with hope, too. I loved meeting her in front of the church before going to school, so that I could apply her lipstick for her, give her the homework I'd copied out and plan for any problems the day might bring. I tried hard not to smudge the lipstick, but it was difficult, because I'd never been very good at colouring in. And the truth is that my heart was also flushed red with love, like the toffee apple we'd shared at the fair, nibbled and gnawed in just the same way, with nothing but a tiny pip in the middle.

I've noticed that when things unravel, it always happens very quickly. Bad luck never seems to arrive one step at a time. I'd almost forgotten about Van Gogh and his ear. But he'd forgotten nothing. You can recognize really mean people by their appetite for revenge. He must have been watching us very closely, figuring it all out from the way we behaved. Then he'd cooked up a plan to separate us and get Marie on her own. Sometimes being mean can make you almost clever.

I realized it was all about to go wrong when Marie held a card out to me one afternoon as we walked towards her house.

"Hey, look, I've been invited to a birthday party. Can you read it to me? I think I should go, or it might seem strange."

I looked at the card. It was blank. Just a plain white card.

"But ... what did you say?"

"Well, I had to reply straight away, so I pretended to read the card. I said I'd come and that I knew how to get there. Now I need to know when and where the party is... Maybe you could come with me..."

Catastrophe. The tsunami of the century. I looked at the little snow-white card that was about to bring us crashing down.

I leant against a tree. In the distance I could hear the sound of the boules clunking against each other and the players congratulating each other on their shots.

"I don't want to alarm you, but I think this is a trap. There's nothing written on the card. Nothing at all."

She was very calm and said nothing at first. She seemed to be thinking it over.

"Is that a problem?" she asked.

Her lack of a grasp on reality nearly blew my mind. As my father always said, running the world should really not be left in the hands of intellectuals. I don't know why, but yet again images from the TV programme about the deportations flickered through my mind. I shook my head to banish them.

"It means that they're out to prove that you can't see anything. They're going to blow the whistle. Believe me, your parents will know about it by tomorrow morning. Maybe sooner."

We walked on in silence.

"You're right. There's no other explanation. What else could it mean? We'll have to face up to it. It's a shame, because we nearly made it. How many days left?"

"Four," I said, angrily holding up four fingers in front of her eyes, not that there was much point in that.

"I'd already chosen my dress for the audition. It's always near the end that you lose concentration. It's a curious tendency, as a matter of fact: the same thing happens in concerts."

"Do you really think all is lost?"

The strange crack in my voice seemed to startle her.

295

"Maybe it won't be so bad after all. My parents will put me in that elite specialist college and I'll be able to study."

"And you're still sure they won't change their minds?"

"Quite sure. They were talking about it only last week. Right from the start they weren't very enthusiastic about me pinning all my hopes on the cello. Music's a high-risk profession! You can be sidelined very quickly. So imagine what they'll think now... But don't worry about me, I'll be able to play music on special occasions, so there we are. You mustn't let it upset you."

She stroked my shoulder, as though I was the one who needed comforting.

"It was a great adventure, though, wasn't it...?" she said.

I began to yell, as though she was deaf as well as blind.

"Don't say that! Listen to me: I swear to you on ... on Dad's Panhard, and on the three musketeers too, I swear you're going to pass the audition! I don't know what we're going to do or how we're going to make it happen, but what I do know is that in four days' time you're going to play your piece and the judges will be in shreds for at least a month, just as people always are when they hear your music. The red carpet will be yours for evermore."

She didn't look convinced by this. But all the same, she said, "You're sweet."

Then we said goodbye, because she wanted to fetch her cello and get to her music lesson. I walked past the church and once more I felt an urge to go inside. To be honest, it wasn't really my sort of place, but desperate times call for desperate measures. I took out a few coins and bought a candle. It shone gently when I lit it, with a slight warmth, and the smoke seemed to rise, coiling, somewhere up above.

By the time I got home I was done in. Dad thought I had a fever – at least thirty-eight degrees, in his opinion. He said anyone would think I'd buried both my father and the Panhard on the same day.

"You've got that look about you again, old mate – like someone who's not cut out for happiness," he said.

I didn't even dare look at myself in the mirror. I wanted to blurt out the whole story, right from the very start, but I held back, because he might have thought the most sensible thing to do would be to tell Marie's parents. Then it really would all be over:

dead and buried with a five-star funeral!

I hardly touched my supper. Dad tried to cheer me up by showing me a book about the history of Panhard cars, with lots of colour photos of saloon cars in the snow, at the seaside, in the city. I listened with half an ear as Dad explained that some PL17s had a revolutionary reclining seat system called "Relmax", short for "relax maximum". I couldn't work up much enthusiasm, but I thought it was good that he had a hobby all the same. Being passionate about Panhards, chess or music, or even collecting things, seems to me like a sort of self-protection mechanism: it helps to keep other people at arm's length and stops you getting too involved with them. That way you can avoid feeling compassion, which is a most uncomfortable emotion.

I brooded all evening. I tried to be methodical, as our teachers were always telling us to be:

What should we fear?

EVERYTHING.

What can we hope for?

NOTHING.

It was as simple as that. There's no denying it, method makes things clear. If Van Gogh was behind this business, he definitely had something up his sleeve. I was going to have to deploy the Nimzo-Indian Defence once again, and develop an understanding of the dangers ahead of us that would exceed the dangers themselves. That's called foresight and it's an essential quality in life. So thanks for that, Mr Nimzovich.

This is where I'd got to with my thinking when I stopped by at Haisam's lodge very early the next morning. My head was bursting: I wouldn't have been surprised if my brain had started coming out through my nostrils. Haisam was setting up his chessboard, very slowly and systematically.

Before he could say anything, I launched straight in.

"Tell me about Nimzovich – you know, the guy who survived by defending himself."

He raised his great head and I could see from his expression that he'd understood everything. He was a bit irritating. He smiled.

"Well now, Aron Nimzovich's great discovery was to recognize the effectiveness of the negative game. Do you follow me?"

"Which means what exactly, if you don't mind me asking?"

"Which means undermining your opponent's moves before thinking about going on the attack yourself. His motto was 'Restrain, block, and destroy!'"

"Good plan. And how did he end up, your Nimzovich?"

"He died in 1935, of pneumonia, stupidly, when he was forty-eight."

In the silence that followed I reflected in a philosophical way that strategies were useless against some opponents, who couldn't be outwitted even by the most intelligent chess grand masters.

I thought my Egyptian had forgotten I was still there, but I was wrong, because after a moment he said in a very low voice, "You're going to get a summons later."

It was hardly a surprise. I'd almost run out of emotions. I was wrung-out like a floor-cloth.

"I knew it. It's checkmate this time."

"No, no. It's the endgame, that's all. Let's just say you've got a slight handicap. Nimzovich will only be useful to you if you bring in Reshevsky as well. Remember that Reshevsky was the master of the endgame."

"The Escape Artist?"

"That's right, the Escape Artist."

I could sense that my venerable Egyptian was trying to tell me something, in his symbolic language. Understanding the dangers + finding an escape route... I jumped to my feet. The school was still empty, apart from the cleaners pushing their trolleys laden with floor mops that looked like dead jellyfish. At that time in the morning it was fairly easy to slip out of school without anyone noticing. I set off back towards the village and saw her at last, walking towards me in that careful, mechanical way of hers. It was weird, because there were other kids on their way to school and I was running against the current, towards Marie. Seeing her from afar, I realized her posture had got slacker and she was being less careful in her movements. I should have noticed much earlier that to everyone else she was getting to look more and more like a blind person. But because I was with her all the time I obviously saw her in a different light. As I ran, I came up with a psychological theory: it seemed to me that as the weeks had passed, Marie had forgotten how she used to move when she was a seeing person. Now she could no longer replicate her old ways. Without being aware of it, she no longer resembled her old self. She suddenly lifted her face towards me. She didn't dare say anything because she couldn't be sure it was me. Yet she never made a mistake: Marie recognized me every time, probably because of her intuition. It's a particularly female trait, or so I've heard.

"Is that you, Victor?"

I always liked to wait a few seconds before replying to see how she'd react. Generally, it didn't bother her much, because she was very self-confident despite her disability.

"Victor, I know perfectly well it's you. You don't frighten me, I can recognize you easily. I waited for you by the church. What are you doing here?"

She pulled a lipstick out of her bag and stretched her lips into a taut, round shape. Like a pale-coloured sweet.

"Listen," I said, "this is an emergency. I was right, the invitation card was a trap. My Honourable Egyptian told me we're going to be hauled in. He knows everything that goes on at the school. Caretakers don't earn much but they pick up on a lot of news. The lodge is like a control tower."

I paused to see how she was taking it. She seemed very calm, almost relieved.

"OK… Here's what I'm going to do. I'll go back home and tell my parents the truth. It'll just take one phone call to the specialist college and everything will be sorted. Chances are, I won't even have to set foot in school again. It's just bad luck, that's all. The loss of concentration towards the end of a concert – it's the biggest pitfall for a musician! The most banal, but the most dangerous!"

Her voice cracked. She bit her lips, leaving little teeth marks.

"To start with, give me your lipstick. That's it … very good … that's better … very pretty. Even when defeat's staring you in the face, you need to look presentable! Now I'm going to tell you something: my Dad watches a lot of historical documentaries on TV. I watch them with him, because we've always done everything together, but that would take too long to explain. Once I saw a documentary about the Jews. The Nazis wanted to put them into these camps and then kill them. This isn't fiction, it really happened. To start with I didn't believe that they made soap out of their fat and pillows from their hair, but Dad explained it was all true."

"I know."

"You knew already?"

"Of course I did. But why are you telling me this? You really are weird sometimes."

"No, listen, there's a connection. Some of the Jews realized straight away that they were going to be transported and even killed. They understood the danger and escaped to all different parts of the world!"

"Yes, OK, and so?"

She didn't seem to understand.

"Are you dumb or what?" I yelled.

I shook her shoulders. She was as light as a doll.

"We have to escape, Marie, and hold out until the audition! Three days and two nights, it's not impossible. Otherwise they're going to park you in a specialist camp and I'll never get over it, on account of compassion and being exiled from you. I've learnt something from Dad's TV documentaries: the best weapon is escape! I don't want us to give up! Not only for you! For me too. Because I used to be completely worthless and now I'm worth a bit more, thanks to you. I'm not talking about all the school stuff, because in the end that's not so important, and anyway I know I'll never be as intelligent as you and Haisam. It's more to do with my spirit. I've reached a slightly higher level in that respect since getting to know you – I've been enlightened, as though a soul had been grafted onto me. If we don't take this through to the finish, I'm going to fall back even further down than I was before. I'll be stuck there until the end of my life, grey with dust, and there'll be nothing more to hope for."

In reply she sneezed, so I handed her a tissue. Her nose was all red and she didn't look all that well.

"But where could we escape to? Have you got any ideas?"

"Yes, I know where we can go. Are your parents at home?"

"No, they're away and they won't be home until late."

"OK, so go home and pack up some warm clothes. I'll come and get you in two hours. First, I just need to take care of someone who needs my help."

"Have you started to specialize in humanitarian actions?"

"Yes, it seems a good secure job."

"What about the cello?"

"What do you mean?"

"Should I bring it?"

"Of course you should bring it."

She was still hesitating.

"And ... um..."

She really looked very worried.

"What?"

"Will I need pyjamas?"

"Pyjamas. Of course we're going to take pyjamas."

Honestly. Artistic types and common sense are worlds apart.

12

My little blackbird looked at me in astonishment and hesitated for a moment, as though he suspected a trap, but couldn't resist the birdseed I'd put down on the paving stones. His little yellow beak, tapping against the stone, shone in the fresh morning sunlight. He hopped a bit further into the yard. He seemed to turn around for a last look, and I realized that a separation was coming. He ruffled his crumpled feathers and I was glad to be setting him free, even if it did mean goodbye.

I was a bit worried about what Dad's reaction would be when he got home. I put a lot of effort into the note I left for him. I said I had to go away on my own to think about the future and life in general. He was very fond of thinking things over himself, so I felt sure he would understand the need for it and that would put his mind at rest. I explained that I couldn't tell him where I was going but that I wouldn't take any risks. I'd be back in a few days' time and then I'd go to El Dorado with him every evening and would always shave first. I underlined the word "shave". I also said I was sorry about the cans of ravioli I was taking with me. I tried to be as reassuring and comforting as possible, but I still had some scruples:

Scruples *a feeling of doubt or uncertainty about the morality or propriety of a course of action; anxiety about a moral issue.*

Marie was probably having feelings of doubt and uncertainty too.

I held her hand and stamped on the brambles in front of her so that her legs wouldn't get scratched. She was carrying her cello on her back, in a case that was bigger than she was. The forest was deep, dark and cool and the cabin hadn't changed, just as Etienne had told me. A little wave of nostalgia took me back to the time we built it… It was a really neat cabin, with its proper door, its four bunk beds and its little kitchen corner. We'd intended to spend several days there, hanging out with our music. But rock music is a bit feeble without access to electricity, so we'd quickly abandoned the idea of an artistic retreat. I just hoped Etienne wasn't planning to bring Warty Toadskin there. We weren't exactly singing from the same songsheet: all they cared about was smooching to the sound of rock music, while my concern was Marie's destiny, stitched together from semiquavers. Just three short days and two nights. Two nights with our fingers crossed. With a bit of luck, Marie's parents might not send out search parties until the next day, or even the day after. It was feasible. And in that case we'd be in with a chance of having the audition sewn up, without running into any obstacles.

"Look," said Marie, rummaging in her bag. "Look what I remembered to bring..."

She held up the piece of paper like a flag and I read the words "Friday, eleven o'clock". I had stage fright already.

"It's the invitation to the audition. Luckily, last week Mum said she'd stuck it on the fridge. My days, Victor, do you really think we're going to make it? Frankly if you can lead me out of this labyrinth, it'll be you who's the real maestro."

"They might track us down before the audition, of course," I said, "but at least we'll have tried our best!"

I arranged the tins in an old crate while Marie felt her way along the walls to get an idea of the space and where she could store things. I got the dictionary out of my rucksack and put Dad's little camping stove on top of it. Marie shook the creases out of an elegant dress and then hung it on a coat hanger, which she attached to an old nail sticking out from the wall.

"Are you going dancing?" I asked.

"It's for the audition, you numbskull!"

I honestly think we were happy. There was silence all around us, just the mysterious life of the forest and the gentle rustle of the wind.

"I wonder if they've noticed we're missing, at school?" she asked.

I looked at my watch.

"Yes, of course. But Lucky Luke will be too busy with his reading to do anything about it straight away. No one will be told before this evening. We're safe at least until tomorrow."

In the afternoon I watched as Marie took out her cello and applied rosin to the bow in long gentle strokes. The glinting lights in her hair lit up the cabin. I tried to hold on to the sight of it, because I felt the time had come for me to lay down some memories: they're far more important for someone like me than anything artistic. As I looked at the instrument I seemed to see my father's face between the strings. One day, he too would be nothing more than a colossal memory. And there's nothing you can do to prevent the sting of time passing. I settled down on a bunk, leaning my chin on my right hand. Marie began to play a piece by Johann Sebastian that I'd already heard before at her house. The bow slithered and weaved over the strings, like a long snake. Now and then it stopped suddenly and the sound of birds calling in the forest filled the silence.

"This passage, do you prefer it if I play it like this?" asked Marie.

I listened.

"Or like this?"

I couldn't tell the difference.

"I just want to know how you'd like to hear it on Friday, that's all."

"The second way then."

"You're right. I agree."

I felt flattered.

Evening came and darkness washed through the cabin. The swaying shapes of the trees kept us company. We were going to have to get undressed and a deep silence came between us. Obviously, I'd thought about this beforehand, but I'd come to the conclusion that naked or dressed, it would be all the same to Marie. But I was wrong: her blindness gave me an even stronger sense that I was being watched. So to preserve our modesty, I separated the cabin in two with a long piece of cloth – though I could still see her silhouette twisting and turning to get into those famous pyjamas of hers. The cello's shadow was also projected onto the wall of the cabin. It looked enormous, almost monstrous, as though it would swallow Marie up in the night. Like the Minotaur in the labyrinth. We listened to the noises of the forest and the trees murmuring to each other while we talked softly to keep our spirits up.

"Do you think they're looking for us?" she asked.

"Not yet. They'll wait to see if we come back on our own. Don't worry, in two days it'll all be over. You know what, Marie?"

"No…"

I hesitated.

"All through this year, you let me share your dream. I won't ever forget that."

It wrenched my heart because what we were going through now would one day become the past. I thought about Dad and how worried he'd be. It's hard to do something good for someone without hurting someone else.

It was the middle of the night when things began to change. The wind whistled and the rain drummed on the roof. The trees all around us started writhing in a sinister way, drenching our shelter with gallons of water. Worst of all, as the night wore on, the temperature dropped sharply, as though the seasons were going backwards. Marie was coughing and wheezing as she breathed.

We woke at dawn, feeling as though we'd been sleeping in a sponge. I was expecting to find mushrooms growing in my socks. The rain continued to beat down on the forest and a freezing fog was rising from the earth. I tried to reassure Marie.

"It's good, it's the best thing that could have happened!"

"Really? I'm cold. And my cello needs flippers."

"Of course it's good, it's going to hold up the search. They'll never come looking for us in this weather."

Marie's cheeks were red and her eyes were shining. I placed my hand flat on her forehead, thinking how comforting it was when Dad did that to me.

"What are you doing?"

"I'm checking if you have a fever."

"And what's the verdict, Doctor?"

"I've no idea, because it's something Dad does and I don't know how to tell."

I heated up a can of ravioli, using a whole army of matches because most of them were swollen with damp and as soft as putty.

Then Marie tried to practise but the cold seized up her fingers. In any case, the sound wasn't coming out right: the cello seemed to have lost its voice.

"It's super sensitive, you have to admit," I said.

"It's a living thing, that's all," said Marie. "It's caught cold."

Then she did something extraordinary. She began to rub the cello, on its belly, on its back, on its sides. She blew into its lungs through the sound holes, just as you'd do for someone who's nearly drowned.

She'd caught cold too. She went to bed and slept through most of the afternoon, wrapped up in her sleeping bag. Her sleep was punctured by fits of coughing, mingling with the sound of the rain beating relentlessly against the trees and dripping through the gaps between the planks of our shelter. It was like being on board the *Titanic*. After the iceberg.

One more night, one more day.

I remembered a historical documentary I'd

watched with Dad about those soldiers in the First World War who'd fought for four years in terrible conditions and who'd then succumbed to Spanish flu on the day of the Armistice, in the middle of all the celebrations.

I was beginning to wonder if we'd have to surrender before the end of the battle, beaten by a simple case of flu that wasn't even Spanish.

That evening she asked me to read her some poetry from a book she'd brought on purpose. I admit there were some nice poems in it, but what worried me was that she wanted to listen to the poetry whilst lying flat on her back. It had a sort of religious feel to it that turned my blood cold. While I was reading, she watched me with a strange frown on her face, her eyebrows quivering slightly. And then she almost coughed her lungs out. At this point I felt like giving up.

"Would you like to go back?"

"Don't be silly, Victor."

I don't know quite why she said that because to be honest I'd never been less silly than I was on that day. And to be honest perhaps just quietly going back home would have been the least silly thing of all.

I wanted to make a hot meal, but I realized that

my calculations had been a bit out: there was only one small tin of ravioli left. And one match. I had a look in the dictionary:

Sacrifice *ritual offering to a deity. The act of giving up something valued for a religious, moral or practical purpose.*

This didn't give me much moral support, but still I poured it all onto her plate. Right then I was hoping they'd already sent out the search parties and were about to smoke us out.

"It's good, your ravioli," said Marie, her voice as hoarse as the cello's.

"It's Dad's favourite meal, especially this brand."

My heart ached because of all the emotions tumbling through me, and also from hunger. But I bottled it all up.

"Yes, it's great," I went on, "in fact I've already cleared my plate."

I found myself thinking that compassion really is a tricky business. It's difficult to have a full heart when your stomach's empty.

In the evening, as night was falling like a curtain, things didn't get any better: Marie threw up all her meal. She was about to go straight back to sleep and

I was only just in time to give her a little shake and say, "We have to go back, Marie. This really isn't working out. You've thrown up the ravioli and you're as white as a sheet. You're ill. You need to be looked after! This place is as leaky as a sieve, it's going to kill you!"

"I'm ill, but I swear it's going to be OK. It's flu or something. Or maybe just stage fright, that'll be it, I think, stage fright... Take my hand, that'll do me good."

I could feel something like a little heart beating *allegretto* in the palm of her hand. It felt like holding my blackbird.

"But don't you understand how feverish you are! And you're shaking like a leaf. At least let me go and get some provisions and medicines. Otherwise, even if we hold out until tomorrow, you're not going to be fit to play... What is it you're going to play, by the way?"

"The prelude to Cello Suite number five."

"By Johann Sebastian?"

"Yes, by Johann Sebastian."

"Right, well, to do justice to Johann Sebastian, you need to be on form. Do you think he'd be happy to see you in this state? With all those children he had and his paternal instincts, he must be keeping an eye on you!"

She nodded and added weakly, "But only if you promise to come back quickly and lie down beside me!"

I left the forest. In the darkness, the torch lit up the shafts of rain with long strokes like a paintbrush. The wet roads were shining brightly, as if they'd been oiled. Perhaps the wisest thing would be to tell someone, Dad if he was there, or even Marie's parents if necessary. Or I should go and bang on Haisam's door. He could forget about parables for once: I wasn't in the mood to hear simple tragedies being talked about in some obscure way. It was clear that Marie was slipping through my fingers, that her last drops of strength were draining away like a stream in the sand. I sat down for a few minutes in a bus shelter and began to cry. I was holding Marie's life as well as her destiny in my hands.

I crossed the village and came to the church. I could see in the torchlight that the door was ajar. I was surprised, because I thought that it would have opening hours, like shops do. What comfort I hoped to find in a place like that I'm not sure but I went inside. There was a sort of light shining at the back and the whole place had a sinister feel. I turned off my torch. From behind, I could see a man laying things out on that table thingy which has a scholarly name I can't remember. After a moment the man turned round.

"Are you crying?"

I wiped my face and nodded.

He sighed.

"All the French players have been eliminated from the French Open Tennis Championships," he said. "It's sad."

This was the last thing I expected and I pinched myself to check I wasn't dreaming. I thought he must be a parabolic priest who expressed himself in obscure ways.

"Is that a parable?" I asked, to show that I knew what was what.

He gave me a strange look and turned back to his table. I could hear the objects tinkling against each other. Suddenly, he turned around to look at me. He appeared to be angry.

"Doesn't it mean anything to you that France has no players left in the French Open?"

"But sir, I can't do anything about it. Nothing

at all. There are times when you can't do anything about what happens."

He seemed to consider this.

"It's true. You can't do anything about it. Nobody can. Our players fought hard, but their dreams came to nothing."

"I'll go now, sir. I think that would be for the best."

"That's a shame, because I think you're compatible."

"Compatible? Compatible with what? You're extremely parabolic, sir."

"Just compatible, that's all. You'll have to come back and we'll run some tests."

I was beginning to feel spooked.

"Tests?"

"We'll have to wait for Wimbledon now. It's annoying. Couldn't you have come earlier? Couldn't you have got a move on? Never mind, you'll be entitled to a full set of tests. Don't worry about it, I've also got a first-aid certificate."

Was I going mad? I ran out of the church as fast as I could, and ended up in the square where the fair had been. I remembered the toffee apple that Marie and I had shared. My legs felt like jelly. I was hungry and frightened. The moon appeared briefly, right up high, and it seemed to be sticking its tongue out at me.

That's when I saw the police car, parked in front of the town hall. The revolving beacon was spraying blue streaks of light into the darkness, etching an unearthly pattern onto the walls of the houses. I was going to get caught for sure, if I tried to make it home.

I turned around, keeping close to the walls. My heart was beating so fast that I thought it was going to jump right out of my chest. I went back towards the forest on tiptoe, as though I was scared of waking up the whole village. Once I was in amongst the trees I felt safer. I was even soothed by the shadows dancing mysteriously around me. In the dripping cabin, Marie was asleep. Her hair was thickly matted with sweat. She seemed so small and lost in her big sleeping bag: she probably weighed less than her cello. I thought about my Honourable Egyptian, who often spoke about "deadlocked positions" on the chessboard. Marie was moaning weakly, as though she was dreaming. I lay down next to her and squeezed her burning hand. She woke up.

"Why are you crying, Victor?"

"No reason, Marie. Anyway, I'm not crying."

"You know, Victor, I'd like to go back on the bumper cars with you..."

"We could have a toffee apple..."

She held me tight in her arms and soon the fever returned. I knew now that all was lost. Even if they didn't find us before the audition, Marie wasn't going to be up to playing Johann Sebastian. He must be feeling gloomy up there wherever he was.

I fell into a deep sleep, dreaming about the mad priest chasing me with a syringe. He was reaching out for me and no matter how hard I fought against it, I was too weak and feeble to resist. Luckily, just as he was about to grab hold of me, Dad arrived like a divine apparition, radiating the solemn aura of ancient times that kept disaster and doom at bay.

"They really don't look too good!" said Dad, lifting me off the bunk.

The dream's bubble had burst. Outside it was broad daylight and sunbeams were shining into the cabin. Haisam and Lucky Luke were taking care of Marie and making her drink. One was supporting her back while the other held the glass to her lips.

"How did you find out, Dad, how?"

"Marie's parents came to see me last night, with the school authorities."

"But how come you found us here?"

"We went to ask Haisam — that was my idea. We'd begun to worry, because of the weather... We couldn't really make out what he was talking about: he began to tell us about a 1956 chess tournament... The breakthrough came when we thought of Etienne and his brother. I was sure they'd have some idea. Etienne remembered the cabin. He's odd, by the way, your friend. It wouldn't surprise me if he ends up in trouble."

"It's nothing serious," I said. "He's in love, that's all, so he's trying to sort out his feelings as best he can. And the police, are they after us too?"

"No need to worry about that. I've sent them packing... Really, you do have some strange friends," he sighed.

"And Marie's parents..."

"They know everything now."

Dad looked up and I followed his eyes.

Marie's parents were standing in the open doorway. Etienne was between them, wearing his Darth Vader costume.

That's it, I thought. *Checkmate.* Marie turned towards me and our eyes met, just as though we could see each other. Her parents were standing motionless, their hostile eyes darting between their daughter and me. Then Marie's father stirred into action and sudenly began to roar.

"Right, that's enough of this farce! Straight to the hospital with you! We're going to get you out of here, Marie. Really, just look at this slum!"

He waved his hand to take in the whole crumbling cabin.

Marie burst into tears. As if possessed by a furious energy, I stood up and started shouting, "No! No! Not the hospital! No way! Dad, you can't let them do this... We've got an audition to pass. Otherwise you might as well leave us here to die, there's nothing else for it."

"An audition?" Dad asked. "Victor, what on earth are you on about?"

"A music audition. To get into music school. Look, the cello's over there. And there's the invitation! I'm the page-turner. It's not an easy job."

Marie's father let out a cackle that was mocking and menacing, but plaintive too.

"When's this nonsense going to end?" he shouted.

He turned towards me and pointed, his finger quivering with rage.

"You... You... You are not going to drag her any

further down this path! Marie, do you realize just how far he's led you? Believe me, later on you'll thank us… Tomorrow we'll visit the specialist college. There you'll have all the chances you deserve. Enough of this fiasco!"

Marie was lying curled up on the bunk, desolate and listless, her back against the wall. Her face was buried in her arms.

I believe that everyone gets to experience fifteen miraculous minutes in their life. Well, this is when it happened for me.

Very slowly, as though staggering under his own weight, my dear Haisam got up from the bunk where he'd been sitting. His big glasses were steamed up and his little eyes looked out of focus. He went up so close to Marie's parents that his belly almost touched them. He stood silently and very calmly in front of them, without a hint of aggression. Then he moved his large face even closer to theirs and asked them to step outside the cabin for a few words.

"Listen, Dad," I said, "if you drive us to the music school, I'll clean your rocker arms every month for ten years. And I'll sweep El Dorado for you every week. If you refuse, I'll never shave again and you'll have a son with a beard. Not the best look for a thirteen-year-old…"

"First, Marie's parents will have to change their minds…"

"Don't worry about that. If Haisam's involved, it's sorted. Believe me, there's no way they'll measure up to him. Whatever he says will tip the scales in our favour! The problem is Marie. We have to find a way of getting her back on her feet before the audition, otherwise she's going to get deported to a specially equipped camp."

"It's true she can't play in that state," said Lucky Luke, running a hand through his thick hair.

"Especially Johann Sebastian," I added. "It's not just any old thing, you know!"

There was a bit more colour in Marie's cheeks, but she was still coughing a lot and shivering with fever. So Lucky Luke, after checking that Haisam was still keeping her parents busy outside, beckoned us all to gather around him. He put his finger to his lips to indicate that discretion was needed.

"Right, I've got an idea, but it's a sensitive matter. Very sensitive. Tomorrow I'm supposed to be in a race. In cycling we often take – how can I put it? – nutritional supplements … to boost our fitness … all quite safe…"

He seemed strangely awkward and it made me think of kids trying to explain themselves in his office.

"I happen to have with me," he went on, "a little bottle of these ... supplements. I was supposed to take them in a few hours' time... But we could give them to her now and she'd be able to hold out then until the end of the audition. I know the right dose ... because I have a first-aid certificate... I've got them right here..."

"Can I have some too?" butted in Darth Vader, in a voice from a distant galaxy.

"No," said Lucky Luke. "You don't qualify. It's only for extreme emergencies."

Marie had only just swallowed the last pill when her parents came back into the cabin. Haisam stayed outside. Very calmly, he was lining up some pine cones on the ground. He'd play chess on Mars, I thought to myself. Time stood still. Nobody said anything.

"Marie, hurry up! Get up and get dressed!" said her father.

Marie seemed to be paralysed, unable to make the slightest movement. We all held our breath.

"Are you going to get up or not?" he said. "Today's your chance. There's a little window of opportunity opening for you. Do we need a crane to lift you up?"

I smiled, because Dad often used the same expression.

Marie's father's face was all contorted, as though he might be about to cry. His wife, behind him, was blubbing like a baby.

"You're looking better at any rate! That's extraordinary!" he added.

"She's ready for the final sprint," said Lucky Luke.

I glanced at the invitation hanging on a nail.

"What time is it now?" I asked.

"Nearly ten-thirty," said Dad.

"LET'S GO!" we all shouted at once.

Dad grabbed the cello and Marie felt for my hand.

We followed each other in single file through the forest. With the tips of his fingers, Lucky Luke was holding the coat hanger that carried Marie's beautiful concert dress. I thought we looked like a band of poachers. And in a way it was true: we were trying to cheat fate.

The Panhard and the big BMW were parked at the edge of the wood. Lucky Luke had left his bike behind them.

Marie changed between the doors of the Panhard. In her floaty white dress she looked like a fairy lighting up the forest.

"I'm going with Victor," she said. "He's my thread, I'm not letting go."

Darth Vader got into the BMW with Marie's parents. Haisam sat next to me in the back of the Panhard and Dad settled Marie into the front.

"I'll follow you!" shouted Lucky Luke, throwing his leg over his bike. "Don't try and shake me off, you'll never do it!"

While he was driving, Dad looked at me in the rear-view mirror, with an expression that seemed both intrigued and concerned.

"What's the matter, Dad? Why are you looking at me like that?"

"You haven't shaved for a week. You don't exactly look your best."

It was incredible how much space Haisam filled in the Panhard. He seemed very relaxed, oblivious to the miracle he'd brought about.

"What on earth did you say to them to make them change their minds? How do you do these things?"

My noble Egyptian just sighed as though I was bugging him. He wasn't going to give anything away.

"Frankly, you're a champion. That's all I can say."

Behind us, Lucky Luke was pedalling at top speed,

leaning into the bends. Head down, with knitted brows, he wasn't going to be left behind.

When we arrived, the first candidates had already performed, but luckily Marie was in the second half of the programme, so we still had a bit of time. We left her in a room where she could focus her mind and warm her fingers up.

"Victor, don't forget to come back in five minutes: I need my page-turner!"

"In the state I'm in? I look like a wild boar."

"Be here in five minutes. Stark naked for all I care!" she said, before disappearing into the rehearsal room.

We all looked at each other, stunned. That wasn't her usual turn of phrase. Maybe it was something to do with Lucky Luke's pills.

"You see," said Dad, "you should have shaved. You have to do things your own way and this is the result!"

The audience for the first half were just leaving. A steward ushered us into the hall. Haisam looked a bit sad. He took a step backwards.

"Aren't you coming to watch?" I asked.

"Bravo, my little maestro," was his only reply.

And then he started to head off towards the exit.

I caught up with him and grabbed hold of his checked shirt.

"You can't leave like this! Not today!"

"I have to! Today … it's the Sabbath."

"You're beginning to be a right pain with this Sabbath and its variable dimensions! Look, you've been in a car, you've been out all afternoon and, for all I know, this evening you'll be eating sausages in front of the TV."

"Exactly. There's no need to make it worse. You know that Reshevsky refused to play chess on Saturdays? Throughout his thirty-year career he always insisted that none of his games should be scheduled on the Sabbath."

"Don't give me any nonsense about your Reshevsky and his quirks. That was up to him! If he wanted to twiddle his thumbs every Saturday, fine! I'm talking about you, Haisam. And you, do you really want to leave?"

He seemed embarrassed. I think it was the first and only time I said something to make him question his conscience.

"Want to leave? No, it's not that. Actually, I'd really like to stay. I can't tell you how much I'd like to!"

At last, it was time. They called Marie and her page-turner. I was expecting to be weak at the knees with my teeth chattering like a metronome, but instead the calm that washed over me seemed to come from the furthest reaches of outer space, as though I was wholly absorbed in the peaceful passing of time.

In the hall, I could see Dad next to Haisam and Lucky Luke. Darth Vader was sitting between Marie's parents. The jury was on our right, set back a little.

Marie seemed to be on another planet. Her eyes were wide open as though she'd been hypnotized.

Gradually, the public quietened down and silence spread out over the room like a blanket. There was a pause. Marie was holding her bow a few centimetres above the strings. I held my breath. I glanced quickly over at Dad, then at Haisam, who was spilling over his seat. I saw him raise his big hand, almost imperceptibly, for my eyes only. Everything that is unsaid between human beings was concentrated in that little gesture. And in the short pause before the bow crashed down onto the strings, all my memories came rolling back to me, in a massive pile up. Marie, alone on the road to the village. Marie on the ghost train. The toffee apple. Marie in the dust with her heart full of grief. Marie's eyes. Marie counting her footsteps.

The music rose above the heads of the audience and floated around the room, intense, ethereal and limpid. I turned the pages from time to time for the sake of appearances. Even with my musical ignorance I could tell that Marie was playing in a different way that day, dangerously, almost losing control, as though on the edge of a void. Together, she and I had also journeyed across a dark void during the course of the year. Now and then, the bow slowed down and it sounded as though the music was climbing a steep slope, straining, almost running out of breath; and then suddenly the notes would cascade down over the other side of the crest, in a frantic stampede.

My heart began to beat double fast because I felt that the slightest thing could bring Marie down. I could see her profile. Her face was shining slightly and her hair was flying in all directions.

And then she struck the strings hard with her bow, three times. There was silence again. The sunlight at the end of the labyrinth. Very slowly, very carefully, Marie lifted the bow away from the cello. We could still hear the flowing melody swirling around us. It felt as though the music's last echoes were fading away along with the last traces of childhood, as the thunderous applause broke out.

While we were waiting for the results, in a little side room, Lucky Luke said that Marie had reminded him of the cyclist Bernard Hinault on a mountain descent in his last Tour de France: so fast, and always on the edge of falling. I hadn't seen the race, obviously, but I got what he meant. Marie was with us, completely exhausted. Lucky Luke's pills must have stopped working.

"You were amazing," she said to me.

She couldn't be doing all that badly if she still had the strength to poke fun at me.

"No, really, it was extraordinary, I'm not joking. I was wondering how on earth you did it..."

"What are you talking about?"

"Well, you turned all fifteen pages at exactly the right moment. You were extraordinary!"

After we'd heard the results and the jury's emotional promise of a great future career for Marie, I got into the Panhard. And then I thought she was probably right: you never quite know how extraordinary you really are. The Panhard started up.

"Now," said Dad, "you need to have a shave."

PASCAL RUTER grew up in the southern suburbs of Paris. There is nothing he loves more than stories, especially ones where life's misfortunes and difficulties are subverted by the absurdity and humour of everyday situations. *A Friend in the Dark* (*Le Coeur en Braille*) is Pascal's first novel for Walker Books.

A Friend in the Dark (*Le Coeur en Braille*) was translated into English by EMMA MANDLEY. Emma worked for a long time in broadcasting before becoming a translator from both French and Italian. Like Pascal, she loves stories.